Scarlet White

A Novel

SUZAN MARION McCLELLAND

A&R Publishing

Based on real events from the author's life.

This is a work of fiction. Names, characters, places, and incidents either are the product of the author's imagination or are used fictitiously. Any resemblance to actual persons, living or dead, events, or locales is entirely coincidental.

Book Cover and Interior Design by Monkey C Media
Edited by All My Best
Copyedited by Andrea Glass
Interior Butterfly vector created by FreePik: www.freepik.com

First Edition
Printed in the United States of America

ISBN: 978-1-7373262-0-5 (trade paperback)
        978-1-7373262-1-2 (ebook)

Library of Congress Control Number: 2021917685

To my sons,
Aidan and Rory

PROLOGUE

How much control do we have over our own destiny? I suppose it could depend on the type of person you are, but unfortunately, it may have nothing to do with how hard you try or even the choices you make.

In the game of life, there are those who make the rules, those who follow the rules, and those who break the rules. Life isn't always fair. Sometimes the dice are loaded, and other times you get lucky and land on the propitious square. You travel across the board confident that your eyes are wide open and your perception is reality, only to discover that another player is holding the trump cards, and all the while you thought you had the upper hand. You have every intention of taking that left fork in the road, because if you go left, that path will lead you to a lifetime of wealth and happiness. But you land on the square that tells you to go right, so you have no choice. In your discourse, you find there is no possible way of getting back on track. The path to success. The path that will lead you to your one and only life-long dream.

You lose. Or do you?

My name is Margee McGuire and *this* is the story of my life.

PART ONE

1

THE VIXEN THEATRE: HOLLYWOOD, 1995

I could hear the commotion from the crowd escalating in the auditorium and couldn't fathom how all the other bands that have ever been in this position survived this level of anxiety. I imagined being home right at this very moment snuggled up on the couch, without a worry in the world, watching TV.

As I began warming up my vocals, Randy played scales on his Les Paul, and Mike was running through his bass riffs. Greg had his sticks in his left hand, eyes closed, meditating. Trevor pulled out a bottle of tequila and poured us each a shot. It went down warm and comforting—the golden whisperer, taming my live-wired nerves.

Ten minutes later, a tall Jamaican with dreadlocks poked his head through our dressing room door. "Everything okay back here?" He raised his hand with fingers spread, "Five minutes."

Trevor handed us each a second shot of tequila. I raised my glass. "I just want to say I really love you guys. You're my family. We deserve this. And we're going to win. Let's go out there and kick ass!"

"Here, here," they toasted.

We were polished and ready to kill because a $75,000 recording contract with one of the biggest record labels in L.A. was on the table for the best band tonight.

We received another knock on the door. The Jamaican peered through once again and solemnly made his announcement. "It's time."

The five of us approached the stage briskly and donned our instruments. Brilliant, high-tech lights flooded the stage. Rich, overlapping Persian carpets were rolled out beneath us. Behind a wall of deafening sound, my life at this very moment seemed all too surreal.

I closed my eyes for several seconds, opened them, and suddenly, miraculously, my anxiety vanished. I was Athena—invincible and prepared to devastate. I was the defender of music wrapped in my armor of silk and chiffon crimson, black cherry Doc Martens, and a ruby red Fender Stratocaster. My psyche was connected to the heartbeat of each individual soul in the auditorium. Their collective energy saturated every cell of my body.

Gradually, the shimmer-sheer navy curtain panel in front of us began to rise. Lights flashed. I whipped my mahogany hair to an explosive audience.

2

KISS
(13 YEARS EARLIER)

The mercury had risen to 108 degrees in the shade as I drove my 1963 Chevy Impala, in dire need of a paint job, to our 3:00 p.m. gig at East Central Regional Hospital. My car had no air conditioning, so on days like this, my routine was to wear my hair in a high ponytail and bring along a wet washcloth to cool my face and neck during the drive. I had placed a towel on the driver's seat to avoid contact with the vinyl, which would have caused my thighs to perspire profusely and decided beforehand to arrive early and apply my makeup after I set up my gear. The D.J. was playing a new song on the radio, which made the drive somewhat pleasurable called "Let's Go" by The Cars.

The facility was easy to locate. It was the only building off the Bobby Jones Expressway surrounded by pine tree woods. I exited the Bobby Jones and drove to the second parking structure toward the back of the building, near the recreation area.

When I entered the gym where our stage was set up, I became aware that the residents here were unique, as a boy in his late teens wearing a football helmet shuffled through the hall in aimless circles. Eddie, our bass player, was already setting up his rig when I greeted him. "This should be interesting," he muttered, as his eyes scanned the room.

"Looks like another Gracewood gig," I replied.

Gracewood, an institute for mental disorders, was a charity gig we played the April prior in downtown Augusta where immediately following our performance, one of the patients cornered me, intent on flaunting his vocal talent with Elvis Presley's "Love Me Tender." His rendition of the King was delivered with such passion that his performance came across as satirical, and I was becoming increasingly uncomfortable as he rounded the second verse. But I was stuck. So I stood there and endured the entire ballad as my band mates fought to contain their laughter.

Our manager had told us that this gig was for charity as well, but I had no other information beyond that. My contract stipulated that I would play two non-profit gigs per year. As it turned out, both gigs were for mental institutions.

Performing for mentally challenged adults had some perks in that sometimes the entertainers are simultaneously entertained. In fact, I believe mosh pit dancing originated right here in Augusta with these East Central patients. Many of these patients believed we were legit rock stars as they'd crash on to the dance floor, arms flailing about, bouncing off one another, until a steward could manage to seize them and escort them away. On the other hand, some of the sedated patients would watch us as though mesmerized by a lava lamp, despondent, with very little emotion or reaction at all.

Our performance came to an end, and I began to tear down my gear when one of the patients, in her late twenties, approached me. Her hair was short and dark with heavily cropped bangs. Large, hard-framed glasses supported thick lenses, which magnified her eyes and made them appear to bulge out of their sockets. A wide

A-line gap between her two front teeth was the focal point of her smile. She stared at me with galvanized designs.

"Hello," I offered.

"Do you love me?" she asked.

Somewhat taken back, yet aware that the guys were listening and waiting for my response, I replied, in a matter-of-fact manner, "Of course."

She continued to gaze at me with that star-struck expression. "You don't love me."

"Well, why would you say that?"

"If you love me, you'll give me a kiss."

Engaged in our dialogue, my bandmates were anticipating my response. *What the heck? She's a little girl, mentally,* I concluded. So from our raised stage, I leaned over to give her a kiss on the cheek, but before I knew it, she grabbed my head with both hands and planted a lover's kiss hard on my lips. What lasted several seconds felt more like an eternity, until she finally released me and ran away. I stood there stunned, then turned around to find my comrades chuckling as they continued to pack up.

3

THE WHOLE OF
THE MOON

was nineteen. The East Central Regional Hospital would be the last gig I'd perform of this nature, because I had other plans. Cliché as it sounds, I had a dream, and while playing in a casual cover band had been good experience, there was no real future in it, or at least not the future I had planned.

It was uncommon to see a girl play electric guitar in the South in 1982, which was why getting gigs had never been an issue. My current band had gigs booked months in advance, and we typically entertained the wealthy every weekend, as well as some weekdays. We performed at posh parties and extravagant functions, including the annual Georgia State Medical Board banquet held in the top floor ballroom of the Georgia Railroad Bank on Broad Street in downtown Augusta—a decadent extravaganza for rich southern doctors, and the sky was the limit. A lineup of silver utensils was placed out for each guest who would be dining on a meticulously prepared seven-course meal. Crystal Waterford glasses in different sizes accompanied each place setting for imported French wines, such as Pouilly Fuissé and Bordeaux, which were carefully chosen by a sommelier to match the course. In a circular entry located just before the banquet hall, a four-foot ice sculpture in the shape of a Koi fish was the center piece on a mahogany round table. Surrounding the ice sculpture were appetizers—miniature works of art—created by a master Japanese chef.

I fantasized about being a guest at one of these lavish events, because there were no silver spoons in my childhood. For now, I was just a small-time musician—an employee—entertaining these Georgian socialites.

I learned to play guitar at twelve, taught by my three older brothers, Daniel, Will, and Kerry. By sixteen, I began performing professionally, and at nineteen I was the eclectic Asian-American girl who performed at every live music venue in Augusta and surrounding areas.

In the South, half-Asian girls like me were not considered pretty. The pretty girls were homebred American, and the prettiest girls had blonde hair and blue eyes. The only thing visibly American about me was my slouch, caused by my lack of confidence and the weight of constantly holding my guitar. As a young girl, I was introverted and handicapped by the trammels of shyness. But when I stepped onto the stage, I felt empowered and pretty, so this was the place I wanted to be. And the only time I would spend an hour in front of the mirror applying makeup or styling my hair was before a gig or concert.

My obsession to write and perform music consumed me. Twenty clueless minutes would elapse in Biology class without a molecule of mental absorption as I wrote lyrics and melodies to a song in my head. I imagined being on stage flaunting my brilliance to a packed amphitheater each time a crazy cool song would blast from a sound system. If I wasn't writing, practicing, or performing music, I was dreaming about it. I was organizing a game plan, laying down the stepping stones that would lead me to this elusive dream.

It was in those daydreaming days of high school when I decided my first task was to form a band and start performing *my* songs— my originals. This endeavor would become a long and arduous journey, peppered with some remarkable experiences, beginning in a funky little shack just forty-five minutes outside Atlanta.

4

PRIVATE IDAHO

Covington, located just east of Atlanta, was a two-hour drive from Augusta on Interstate 20. I unzipped and fumbled though my beat-up cassette caddy to retrieve my *Dog and Butterfly* album. I had long idolized Ann and Nancy Wilson. Sometimes, in my sleep, I had dreams that I'd meet the Wilson sisters and we'd become great friends.

The title cut, "Dog and Butterfly", was my favorite song at the time—a sublime ballad that paints a picture of a dog, playfully jumping up after a butterfly which it never captures. My interpretation of the song was about enjoying the journey even if you never reach your goal. A concept which seemed fine, poetically, but through my hungry young eyes, life was all about getting the carrot.

I made the pilgrimage to Jack and Ellie's practically every weekend. Jack and Ellie had gone to college with my brother Kerry prior to Kerry's transfer to Berklee College of Music in Boston. Jack played drums and Ellie, keyboards. The drive was mundane, as the freeway cut through miles of pine tree flatland, typical of Georgia. Hemmed in on both sides by the endless tree line, the only thing to see was the road ahead, and the music made the miles slip by, nearly unseen.

Once I turned onto the Covington exit, I used landmarks as guidelines to direct me to my destination—a right at the textile plant, a left at the water shed, drive another five minutes, cross a small bridge, round the bend, and there it was—the brown shack—the home of Jack and Ellie Stone.

Jack and Ellie's 500-square-foot dilapidated home, located fifty yards from the road, was surrounded by woods, and beyond that, farmland. The front porch supported a rusted tin roof, and the wood siding desperately needed a new coat of paint. But the deteriorating wood would remain exposed to the elements, because purchasing musical equipment was more of a priority.

The front porch was occupied by no less than eighty potted plants that hung from plastic containers or rested on stumps and rusty pedestals. In the back yard, Jack had constructed a 40' x 40' chain-link fence kennel for five dogs, all of which barked at the slightest disturbance in their environment. Ellie had a soft heart. She took in every stray dog that happened to be fortunate enough to wander onto the property. Jack complained and made ongoing demands, "No more dawgs!" But Ellie ignored him, and Jack didn't have the heart to turn the immigrants away either, so the Stone family continued to grow as the years passed. In the side yard, Jack had a garden that produced the best homegrown tomatoes I'd ever sunk my teeth into. He also grew corn, okra, and green beans. The plants that crowded the front porch were also a product of Jack's green thumb. And further, much further, deep into the woods, Jack's pride and joy was a small hemp garden of the finest Columbian Gold ever to cross the border.

3566 Alcovy Road holds a special place in my heart. Although rundown and decrepit, I had grown to love that humble dwelling. Beyond the front door, the tiny living room was on the right and the kitchen on the left. A kitchen peninsula separated the kitchen from the living room—our rehearsal area. A black potbelly stove situated in the living area heated the entire home in the winter. Band equipment packed the remainder of the living room space, wall-to-wall. Ironically, thousands of dollars' worth of state-of-the-art musical equipment decorated this poor man's cabin.

The back half of the house was separated from the front half by a threshold. Beyond the threshold was a small foyer just a few steps from the back door. To the left of the foyer was a bathroom, and to the right, Jack and Ellie's bedroom.

The bathroom was old and corroded, especially the shower. Cracked, stained, and moldy, it had gone years, maybe even decades, beyond its normal lifespan. Had the shower been a human, it would have been dead and buried for quite some time. You definitely had to wear flip-flops to use it. But warm water flowed through the showerhead, and I didn't mind. I was happy and comfortable at the Stone's.

Shortly after my arrival, Ellie prepared lunch for me. I devoured two home-grown tomato sandwiches with mayonnaise, salt, and pepper on bleached white Colonial bread. Sweet, sun-brewed iced tea paired perfectly with my sandwiches.

Once the dishes were cleared away, it was time to break out the instruments and make some music. And it was that music that transformed a ramshackle house into an electric sound garden.

5

HOW SOON IS NOW?

Band practice lasted about four hours, and twice a month Jack and Ellie hosted bonfire shindigs where all the party people of Covington, age eighteen to forty, showed up at sunset with meat for the BBQ, potato and macaroni salads, cases of beer, and some home-grown weed.

Acoustic music by the fire intermingled with bouts of laughter could be heard by surrounding neighbors. And as the night wore on, drink-in-the-hand dancers grooved to a cranked-up stereo blaring The Smiths, Thompson Twins, B-52s… until the police shut us down. The highlight of the evening was when Jack got hammered and performed his signature dance to "Burning Down the House" by The Talking Heads. Springing up randomly, as if he'd gotten an electric jolt, Jack's arms would flop about like a ragdoll. I always thought he was going to stumble and fall, but he never did. We laughed hysterically—except Ellie who would eyeball Jack with a glare of disdain, because she knew what mischief was coming next: the kissing. Once Jack reached his "dancing level" of drunkenness, it was only a matter of time before he would try to kiss every pretty girl at the party.

That was most nights, but not this night. Tonight, there would be no party. Ellie and I would collaborate at the kitchen table instead.

Ellie, a tall girl with wavy brown hair and a strong drawl, pulled out a bottle of Jack and placed it on the table.

"Jack Daniel's?" I grinned. "I thought we were working tonight."

"All the great musicians write their best songs over a bottle of liquor."

Not wanting to buck tradition—and wanting to be among the "great musicians of the world", I shrugged. "Okay," I chuckled, as this type of ritual seemed a little out of character for Ellie. But I was beginning to think maybe I didn't know her character as well as I thought I did.

She poured us both a shot. "Clink and drink."

So we did.

Forty-five minutes into our collaboration, I became aware of a strange noise. It was as audible as a person sitting right next to me crunching on peanut brittle. It was the sound of a creature gnawing away at the house. I looked at Ellie, confused. "What the hell is that?"

Ellie leaned over and banged her fist on the kitchen cabinet below the sink. "Dirty rat!"

"What? You gotta be kidding me. That's a rat?"

"Yeah, we haven't been able to get rid of him. He's a smart one."

"But it sounds like a bigger animal. Are you sure it's not a 'possum or a raccoon?"

"No. That's Billy Bob. He's a rat. Don't worry. He's just looking for dog food."

Ellie's attitude toward this mutant rat was so cavalier, I had to laugh. "Jesus, Ellie... I'm sleeping on the floor...in my sleeping bag...not that far from that thing."

"But he's under the house."

"Sounds like he's right there." I gestured towards the sink. "I heard those guys can skinny-down and squeeze through cracks."

Ellie considered my consternation and let go an exasperated sigh. "Jack's gotta get rid of that damn rat. You can sleep in our room. Jack and I will sleep out here."

About 3:00 a.m. I was awakened briefly by Jack's outburst. Groggy from the J.D., I returned to my slumber.

The following morning, Jack shared an interesting story. During the night, he had a dream that he was getting a tattoo on his neck, but the dream transitioned into a nightmarish reality when Jack was gradually drawn out of REM by the pain of Billy Bob nipping at the back of his neck. Jack whipped around and was face-to-face with Billy Bob when Jack cried out in horror, spewing a stream of obscenities. Billy Bob retreated, raced back to the kitchen, and took refuge through the open cupboard below the sink.

Jack, now obsessed with the extermination of Billy Bob, cut Sunday rehearsal short. Outfitted in camouflage fatigues, a hunting hat, and a rifle—which somehow made me think of a young Elmer Fudd only with wavy shoulder length hair—he relentlessly pursued the varmint. That was my first real peek at a side of Jack I'd never seen before—the unyielding hunter. I was amused.

But it was another side of Jack's personality, the intoxicated kisser, that brought our band, Corrugated Velvet, to an end. In all fairness, Les, our bassist, was the first to initiate the downfall. His wife had been complaining for months that he was dedicating too much time to the band. Due to the relentless pressure at home, he quit.

That was the first nail in the coffin. The final blow came from the two people I so loved and admired—Jack and Ellie. Being in a band and a marriage had its trials and tribulations. The two had started bickering nonstop. On a thunder and lightning-filled Thursday, as the rain pelted down on my rooftop, I got the phone call. It was over. Jack's philandering and procrastinating had finally eaten through Ellie's patience, and that was it.

While it was hard on Ellie, for me it was almost as painful. No more trips to Covington. No more party jam sessions. No more creative evenings over shots of Jack Daniels. No more Corrugated Velvet. I was kicked out of that comfortable nest and left with limited options. The one I finally took was to leave my home town, travel across the country, and seek new levels of music.

But the Jack and Ellie experience was my very first lesson on the negative repercussions of having intimate relationships within the band. I'd seen it happen in other groups. Relationships gone bad create rifts. Rifts create negative vibes, destroying the unity that had once held the band together. Inevitably, one or more members quit, and the band collapses. Alternating between disgust and great disappointment, I sat morosely, thinking of the consequences of Jack and Ellie's relationship. And Les, whose wife demanded that he lay down his guitar and his love of music for her. It didn't seem fair. And here I was. Back to square one. Forced to start all over again. A flashing red light screamed the lesson to my brain. *NEVER*, it shouted, *NEVER have a relationship with a member of the band! And never take on a significant other until after my musical career is established.*

So now I had to hit the restart button. I auditioned for other bands locally, but after a year with no success finding the right combination of musicians, I realized that the pickings were slim for forming an alternative rock band in the South. More importantly, I came to accept that Augusta wasn't the ideal place to land a record deal anyway.

In the spring of 1985, I decided to go west. Two of my brothers, Will and Kerry, had already migrated to Orange County, and I figured having a safe and friendly place to crash while I explored the music scene would make my transition easier. So I gathered my belongings and moved to Southern California where the opportunities and prospects were said to be bountiful.

6

GOING TO CALIFORNIA

I emerged from the jetway to the airport terminal in LAX and immediately spotted my brothers, Will and Kerry. We greeted each other with broad smiles and warm hugs, and Will took my carry-on.

My brothers bantered me as we headed to baggage claim, swapping tales and laughing a little too loud. Will, the older of the two, was unassuming, with short clean-cut hair. He wore a T-shirt, fitted shorts cut just above the knee, and leather slide sandals. I smiled to myself and thought, *He hasn't changed much since the last time I saw him.*

Kerry, on the other hand, had changed considerably since the last time I saw him two years ago. His hair had grown two-thirds of the way down his back, and he was wearing a pair of loose, faded denim overalls with a bare chest underneath, black Converse high-tops, and Oakley sunglasses.

Kerry ushered us to his girlfriend's minivan. We loaded my baggage and piled in as Kerry slipped behind the wheel. On the drive to Orange County, he gave me his guided tour of the 405

Freeway and filled me in on SoCal lifestyle. "You see this carpool lane, Margee? I've driven ninety in this lane." I imagined driving that fast, so close to the concrete wall, cars whizzing by just one lane over as Kerry continued to educate me. "This is the 405 freeway. The 405 and the 5 are the two main freeways that you'll use. Traffic's not too bad today, but sometimes it could take over two hours to get from L.A. to Huntington Beach if it's rush hour. And if there's an accident, it sucks, because every single person who drives by has to look."

"But why? Why do they look if it causes such a delay for hundreds of people?" I asked.

"Because most humans are idiots with no life, so car accidents are a form of morbid entertainment. Also, there's the monkey see, monkey do factor. If one person slows down to look, everybody else has to. I don't give a shit about what it looks like. I just keep my head straight, so I can get where I'm going, but I must be the only one. Life is fast out here, Margee. It's not like Georgia." He glanced over his right shoulder, then made a heart-stopping maneuver to get through a solid line of cars to begin his exit from the HOV lanes.

"What do you mean?" though I was beginning to get the idea.

"There's always something going on, things to do, people to see, more work, more play, more bands, more competition. People drive faster, talk faster, walk faster. Wrote a song 'bout it. Wanna hear it? Here it go." Kerry proceeded to belt a vocal sample. "It's a rat raaaace." He sang in the vocal style of Ozzy Osbourne infused with all the passion of Jack Black—two beats per word, five beats on race. Will and I looked at each other with dolphin smiles.

Then Kerry cranked up the radio and sang along with Poison as I gazed out the window and marveled at the palm trees and billboards that lined both sides of the freeway—KNAC Radio and Corona Beer.

"Welcome to California," Will said from the back seat. We both let go a laugh.

7

KICKSTART MY HEART

The photographer was a mature woman. She focused, zoomed, and directed them. "Strike a pose, boys." And the band posed with hands on hips, heads cocked, and lips puckered.

It was a perfect day for photographs. As we call it in SoCal: June gloom. It looks like it wants to rain but can never commit. I decided to tag along with Kerry's band, Dude Ranch, for their photo shoot in an industrial section of Los Angeles. Kerry's hair was teased extra big, and he was wearing snakeskin print spandex leggings with a black leather vest over a bare chest. A long sparkly silver scarf draped around his neck, and on his feet he wore mid-calf black cowboy boots with pointy toes. His face was made up with eyeliner, eye shadow, blush, and lipstick, topped off with a beauty mark on his right cheekbone.

An important quality for a dude in a heavy metal band is narcissism, which Kerry possessed a measure of. His confidence and charisma were both a product of his narcissism. Most would not notice or care when he would dominate a conversation without an inkling of interest in the other person. After all, who could be more interesting than Kerry McGuire?

Kerry was very much into the heavy metal scene and proclaimed with certainty that heavy metal was the future and that there was no market for any other music. "No one listens to alternative, country, or jazz anymore." He lived in an isolated world of heavy metal. His entire cognition—what he saw, heard, felt, and smelt—was heavy metal. If he walked down a boulevard with all sorts of people—a man in a business suit, or a woman with a Dolly Parton hairdo—his eyes could only see the head bangers.

Shortly after my relocation to California, Kerry decided to change his name to Cory. His real name, you see, wasn't cool enough to match his personality.

On first impression, one could make the assumption that Kerry (or Cory) was your everyday run-of-the-mill, dimly lit, rock musician but quite the contrary. In high school, he was a prodigy classical guitarist, winning highest recognition awards in state competitions three years in a row. I recall waking up in the middle of the night hearing Segovia and Christopher Parkening from the basement just below my bedroom, where he'd practice, some days obsessively, up to twelve hours non-stop. He earned a scholarship to Berklee College of Music in Boston, Massachusetts, and graduated with honors.

Afterward, he became a full-fledged jazz guitarist, but he was struggling to make ends meet. So he relocated to California and somehow changed course. He ended up playing heavy metal and working for extra cash as a part-time chef at a gourmet burger cafe in Huntington Beach, where he invented the Buffalo Bruschetta Burger made with fresh buffalo mozzarella cheese, basil, and thin strips of his spicy hand crafted Italian sausage, topped with a secret parmesan dressing. It was insanely delicious.

In the '80s, L.A. was indeed a depot for heavy metal and glam metal rock bands, which would explain his tunnel vision. The atmosphere, I must admit, also had an influence on me. Cory formed a heavy metal band called Spit Fire. But the guitarist's addiction to heroin took its toll on the band. So Cory formed another band called Hammerhead, still, with no success.

During a cattle-call in Los Angeles, he auditioned for a female lead singer/guitarist who was on the rise. I'll call her Lisa Mustang to protect her anonymity and myself for possible litigation. Previously, she played lead guitar in a short-lived band of young girls. I won't reveal the name of the band, but it rhymes with The Funaways. Another band member of The Funaways become a huge success. She had "jet" black hair. I'll call her Jane Jetson. Jane Jetson had a mega-hit single. The name of the hit track sounds like "I Love Rock 'n' Soul."

A cattle-call is a broadcast announcement calling all musicians—bass players in this case—to audition for a hot new act. It's a real magnet for budding artists like Cory, because it's complete with management, agents, recording contract, tours, and so forth. Aspiring musicians would line up for blocks to audition. Cory was somewhere near the end of the line, usually a bad place to be. But a screener walked the line and pulled auditionees strictly by looks. She gave him a once-over, pointed a pen at him, and said, "You. Come with me."

The next time I saw Cory, I asked, "How'd the audition go?"

"I didn't get the gig," He grabbed a beer from the fridge and flopped down on the couch across from me.

"What was Lisa Mustang like?" I tried to act nonchalant and turned a page of my magazine. Despite myself, my body was leaning forward to mop up every morsel of his description.

He shrugged. "She's a cunt."

And that was the end of the conversation. Best to leave well enough alone.

8

NOTHING BUT A GOOD TIME

Will and I sat in an upper level booth towards the back of the club. The Hot Spot, located in Huntington Beach, was well known for showcasing local live bands. It was early February, and the venue was dark and dank with an overcast of cigarette smoke that seemed to drift in pockets like a band of ghosts waiting for the show.

Most of the tables were empty on this night, but depending on how hard the band promoted their gig, the Hot Spot could be packed like a Tokyo subway during rush hour.

Dude Ranch would be headlining soon, because the opening band had just finished their set. Under the dim lights, we could see Cory and his bandmates tuning their instruments. Each band member made eye contact with the lead singer and nodded. In turn, the lead singer gave a thumbs up to the soundman to give the introduction.

"Alright everybody, please welcome to the Hot Spot, Dude Ranch!"

We cheered for the band. The lead singer's hair was massive and waist-long, thinning out at the ends. His spandex leggings punctuated his frontal package. Their intro was completely choreographed, something you would never see in a heavy metal band. I was impressed, grinning ear-to-ear as I watched this totally unexpected piece.

The songs were a hybrid of heavy metal and pop with classic shout choruses, lots of hooks, speed leads, high pitched vocals, and a loudness that punched you right in the face. The lead singer carried a zealous strut from one side of the stage to the other pointing his finger at the audience and thrusting his fist in the air, doing all the things that any proper heavy metal front man should do.

Cory was every bit as entertaining, whipping his hair up and down. Even as he jumped from table to table, he still had all the moves. He thumb-slapped the strings on his bass, and the fingers on his left hand reminded me of spider legs racing up and down the neck of the guitar. Dude Ranch was forty-five minutes of ear adventure and eye candy.

Over the course of two years, Dude Ranch played many gigs. As hard as they tried, they never got discovered, and the band eventually fell apart.

I tried to convince Cory to join forces with me. He was a ferociously talented bassist with heaps of charisma, but he had reservations about backing up a girl unless of course, she was bona fide by a record label. "It's like this, Margee. When you have a band of guys like Motley Crew; even though the lead singer stands out, each band member is special. But when you have a female vocalist fronting the band, the guys become the backup band, forgotten, insignificant."

While he was somewhat justified in this rationale, I felt his mentality was self-defeating and trivial, because in the big scheme of things, getting signed by a major record label was like winning the lottery. A band has a better chance of getting struck by lightning. While there are thousands of bands, only a meager handful will be picked up by a major record label. A more viable business rational would have been to go with a band that had great songs, an extraordinary stage presence, and most importantly, a fresh new approach. And this, I had come to realize, would be the strategy for my band.

During the '80s, L.A. had a cancerous overflow of heavy metal bands, so by being heavy metal, you actually reduced your chances of success. You were just another heavy metal band, piled on top of all the other heavy metal bands. But Cory, though brilliant in his own right, didn't have a keen sense of intuition. He was only able to grasp the moment, not the future. And for the moment, in his perspective, heavy metal was all there would ever be.

It was during these times spent observing Cory's life in the rock world and his stage persona with all his charisma and magnetism, that I learned lessons. But, along with his glamour and spark, I witnessed his mistakes and oversights. I soaked in an abundance of information, took mental notes, and knew exactly what to do and what not to do. And while I learned a great deal, nothing would prepare me for what I still had not learned. Lessons that only experience could teach. Lessons that could only be learned through my hardest fall and my biggest heartbreaks and disappointments, which were yet to come. These would become life lessons that would transcend beyond the material world and completely reverse my perspective of what is real.

9

A CONNECTION
IS MADE

"**A**re you fucking kidding me? You're getting married? Just like that! Do you know what you're doing? You're fucking us all over, Shenin! You'll live to regret this." Darcy slammed the phone down and threw her hands to her head. She grimaced, but her ego wouldn't allow her to cry. Instead she held the tears inside. And those inner tears fueled the ticking bomb in her head. She rushed to her room, and reached under her bed until her hand could grasp the bottle of Crown Royal.

The Phones were just one signature away from being signed by Virgin Records. But the deal was never sealed when lead singer, Shenin Powell, chose marriage over the band in the final hour. Bassist and back-up singer, Darcy Denikin had never forgiven her.

Months later, when the smoked cleared, Darcy and the remaining band members decided not to hire another lead singer. Instead, Darcy took over lead vocals. Since Darcy had always been the sole songwriter, the band was able to continue, and Darcy, in her new role as lead singer, enjoyed being in the limelight.

But four years passed with no label interest, so The Phones finally decided to add a new lead singer back to the mix to try and recreate what they had lost. And this is when I came into the picture.

When I auditioned, Darcy was stoked that I played guitar, because she was keen to continue singing lead vocals on her songs. As it turned out, my vocals paired perfectly with hers. Darcy was also a gifted songwriter. In the same genre as The Go Go's, Darcy's songs were fun, hooky, and upbeat. But, The Phones were more technical than the Go Go's. With the introduction of my songs and harmonies, and Reed's guitar work, we were sounding like the B-52s riding the Crazy Train. We had a hard edge. And the visual appeal of two female musicians fronting the band was a definite plus.

10

CANNONBALL

My eyes were on a continuous journey in Darcy's garage which had been converted into a rehearsal studio more than a decade ago. The walls were several layers thick with posters, pictures, flyers, stickers, and memorabilia galore. Among the paraphernalia were gas masks, Halloween decorations, and an antique police hat. Colored, vintage Christmas lights illuminated the studio just enough to give it a weird but wonderful glow. Darcy was at the workbench rolling a joint when I arrived with my guitar case in hand and gig bag over my shoulder. "Reed! Mitchell! Don't just stand there," she ordered. "Give Margot a hand with her equipment!"

Reed greeted me with the smile of a little boy who just saw his new puppy on Christmas day. The guys jumped at Darcy's command to fetch my gear.

"Would you like a beer?" Darcy asked.

"Sure."

She handed me a Sapporo.

"My favorite beer."

"I know." Darcy eyed me seductively, head tilted.

I felt slightly intimidated. "So, how are you?"

"Better now that you're here. I got a nice phone call from my country boyfriend today." She lit her joint, took a hit, and extended the offer to me.

"No thanks. I never could mix and match."

She smiled broadly, exhaled, and coughed a bit.

I was curious about her comment about her country boyfriend, because I assumed that Darcy was lesbian. Also, at the Phones' concert where I met Darcy, she was with a girl named Mel, who emanated a strong jealous vibe towards me. Mel's insecurity was in a chronic state of inflammation due to their one-sided relationship. She worshiped the stage Darcy walked on, but at times, Darcy treated Mel like dirt. One evening, Mel showed up at rehearsal to bring Darcy some homemade cookies that she had just baked. Irritated, Darcy humiliated her in front of the band. "Go home. You know you're not supposed to be here."

I felt terrible for Mel, and Darcy sensed it.

"What?" Darcy blurted. "She comes here when she's invited. We're rehearsing."

Not long after joining The Phones, I noticed Darcy's personality flipped from one moment to the next. And she began to flex her muscle more often to maintain her status as the alpha female in the band, displaying episodes of an arrogant and condescending version of herself. Because I used a tuner to tune my guitar rather than tuning by ear, she made a derisive comment. "Real musicians don't need tuners."

In the beginning, I offered no defense to her derogatory remarks and ignored them. Although I knew how to tune by ear, the tuner was a standard tool amongst most rock musicians by 1984. It allowed a musician to tune dead-on to 440 in record time without sound coming out of the amp. A huge asset at gigs and a convenience at rehearsals. As time passed, it was becoming clear that Darcy was stuck in a time warp, living in the past and feeling some insecurity with me in the band.

During the early '80s, Darcy's band had performed in a lineup with The Go Go's at the Pacific Amphitheater, and two of her songs were featured on KROC during Local Licks. This was a high point in her life. Darcy was quick to drop names of all the celebrities she had met and shared stories of those glory days. In her rehearsal studio hung an autographed strat given to her by her celebrity friend, John Stamos. Her main objective was to impress, and in the beginning, she was successful. But as time passed, I came to see her for what she really was—washed up.

Mrs. Denikin was a single mom who supported Darcy for years and prayed that her daughter would "make it" one day. But Darcy didn't have the motivation or a strategy to make it happen. During the day, she didn't do a whole lot, except smoke dope, socialize with other deadbeats, and occasionally pick up a guitar to play or write a song. Over the past four years after the original Phones disbanded, her heavy use of drugs and alcohol had turned her youthful image, immortalized in old photographs, into something quite the opposite. Nonetheless, Darcy saw a goddess standing in front of her mirror: the same Darcy Deniken in those old photographs. And her confidence was an excellent cover for any shortcomings.

While I had a vision of what we could become and how far we could go, I found it difficult imagining a life with Darcy. She was satisfied with treading water. With every idea that I pitched to take the band to the next level, she'd squash it down like a rotten fig.

We agreed to split singing lead and song writing, fifty-fifty. Though Darcy didn't have my double octave range, she had a seductive tone. It was deep, rich, and sensuous. However, an issue needed to be addressed. Who would stand in the middle when we performed on stage?

Because we were a four-piece band, one of us had to stand over to the side. At first, she recommended that we take turns—alternate standing center stage.

"Look, Darcy, I don't mind standing to the side," I suggested.

But the rest of the band preferred that I take the center stage, and they let it be known. And if that wasn't enough, Darcy's sound engineer, Tom Nash, whom she highly respected, dropped in to see us rehearse one evening and gave his input. "Margee plays the guitar. She should stand center stage." While Tom's suggestion was delivered diplomatically, it added another blow to Darcy's ego—an ego that was inflated with toxic smoke, same as her brain for the better half of the day.

Darcy got high before and after rehearsal. During rehearsal, she drank. When rehearsals ended, she was lit. She reminisced and shared stories of her heydays with The Phones which included sex parties.

A mere six weeks after my joining the band, Darcy began doling out sexual innuendos towards me at every opportunity. It was difficult to decipher whether she was making a joke or testing the waters, nevertheless, at age twenty-five, I was uncomfortable with her comments.

It had become tradition for The Phones to perform every Halloween, which was several weeks away. Darcy was persistent at each rehearsal to know what I was going to dress up as.

"I hadn't really thought about it much," I finally submitted. "I'll probably wear a black cat costume. Why do you need to know?"

"Because I can't decide what I'm going to be until you tell me what you're going to be first. If you're going to be a cat, then I'm going to be a litter box."

The guys chuckled.

Though embarrassed, I pretended not to be and laughed with them. "Here we go."

I took into consideration that I could be hyper-sensitive. We were a rock band, after all. Musicians have a tendency towards raunchy humor. Maybe I just needed to lighten up, and I wanted to give Darcy a fair chance. On first impression, I was swept off my feet by all Darcy's talk and hype. Her bio was, after all, impressive, *and* she had a published song featured in a B-rated teen movie. Though it had been several years, she continued to receive small royalties for the song. But Darcy's snide remarks and sexual innuendos were piling up. And I was no longer enjoying being a member of The Phones.

Darcy didn't have a clue about my growing resentments, and any discussion would have been futile because Darcy was a narcissistic bully. Had I opened the door to discussion, she would have scoffed, rolled her eyes, and patronized me. I wasn't about to give her that opportunity. However, my self-preservation mode took off in high gear, and I began to set boundaries. I'd block and counter with a hard hook each time Darcy threw a jab. But in my heart, I was still that starry-eyed naive girl from Georgia. I wanted it to work out with The Phones. To my surprise, Darcy began to back down, but her heavy use of alcohol would drown her inhibitions, provoke her exploitative nature, and awaken the jealous hyena inside. The final straw came one evening after Darcy had way too much to drink, and she crossed the line.

Reed was celebrating his twenty-eighth birthday at his cousin's house, and we had enough songs worked up to play a fifteen-song set. Midway through the night, after our performance, Reed and Mitchell were playing pool in the game room, and I was sitting at the bar outside with a crowd of people around. Darcy sat next to me at the bar. The music was loud, and the people were loud. No one was paying attention to us, and Darcy was intoxicated. "I just thought you should know Mitchell and Reed have a crush on you."

I wasn't sure what to make of this comment. Mitchell was married, and Reed had often joked with me about he and I getting married. From the first rehearsal, Reed, wearing a big smile on his face would tease, "You know, the girl lead singer and lead guitarist always get married." I would brush it off as a joke, because the statement was hardly accurate.

As Darcy continued, I was beginning to wonder if she was thinking about having an orgy within the band, which made me feel extremely uncomfortable. Darcy didn't for a moment detect or consider my mortification. "I like you too, Margee." And this was when her hand slipped down to my upper inner thigh, close enough to my crotch that if she took a sharp right turn, she'd be on home plate. In fact, her pinky was on home plate. I took her hand and placed it on her lap. Without saying a word, I got up and left the party.

A week later, when I didn't show up at rehearsal, Darcy called me to shovel out a tongue-lashing that lasted almost ten minutes. Darcy could not remember putting her hand up to my crotch. She had blacked out. She adamantly denied doing it and continued chastising me as I sat at the other end in silence until she was completely out of words.

"Are you done, Darcy?"

"Yes. What do you have to say for yourself?"

"Nothing." *(Click)* I hung up the phone. And I never heard from Darcy again.

11

JUST LIKE PARADISE

"Dude, she wants to buy this poster of David Lee Roth. He's got no shirt on, and he's pulling his pants down below his hips to the root of his penis."

It was late July when I entered the rehearsal studio for my audition with Crystal Image. Following initial introductions, I was struck by the wall-to-wall posters of scantily clad women, some with wet T-shirts, others with exposed breasts, even a twat here and there, and of course, the well-known Haulin' Ass poster. *Hmmm,* I thought. *If I'm going to be in a band with young dudes, I will have to fit in.* But there had to be compromises. Before accepting my invitation to join the band, I stipulated that I get a spot on the wall to display one of my posters.

On a crisp and clear Saturday morning, I browsed the Orange County swap meet and found the perfect poster—a life-size image of David Lee Roth wearing gauntlet gloves and barely anything else. It was beyond amazing.

"Uhhhh…okay, before you buy that poster, let me talk to the guys," Randy requested.

When I entered the rehearsal studio on Tuesday, the walls were completely bare. Following Randy's description of the poster to the band, the boys took every single nudie picture down. I never bought the Roth poster, but his image will forever be etched in my memory.

12

BEHIND THE WALL OF SLEEP

recognized Randy's silhouette through my window shade as he walked to the front door. A second later, the doorbell rang. I opened the door to find Randy with a big smile on his face, holding a bouquet of flowers.

"Randy, what are you doing?" I asked.

"Every pretty girl should have flowers in the spring."

I reluctantly accepted the flowers. "Thank you. Come in."

Minutes passed, but Randy's smile remained frozen on his face. Feeling a little creeped out, I spoke up. "Randy, do you have something devious up your sleeve? Because when you keep smiling like that, you remind me of the Joker."

He busted out laughing. "No. Just having a good day I guess."

I spent a great deal of time with Randy, learning his songs. Because Randy's songs were already established by the other band members, it made sense in the beginning to learn his music, then incorporate my songs along the way.

Back then, I had not yet experienced life long enough to learn how wrong it was to judge a person when I had not walked in their shoes. As a little boy, Randy faced his father's tyranny and criticism on a daily basis. These verbal assaults eventually caused Randy to stutter. When Randy stuttered, his father became more agitated, only to aggravate Randy's impediment. Randy's solace became his guitar. His songwriting became his therapy, and he managed to cure his stutter himself by spending hours alone in his room with his instrument, writing songs, and mastering the guitar. When Randy played lead guitar, he was nothing short of phenomenal. On stage, he was confident—flawless. But off stage, he could be awkward and pretentious without his musical shield.

Weeks passed, and Randy seemed more relaxed during our sessions. His awkwardness subsided; however, it was becoming apparent that Randy was developing feelings towards me. "Stick with me Margee. We are going to go places together."

"You have to understand, Randy, our relationship will always be strictly professional. Romantic relationships compromise the success of the band. I, personally, will never ever consider having a relationship with a band member."

"Oh yeah," Randy professed. "Tell me about it. I couldn't agree more."

Even if the band were taken out of the equation, I had absolutely no attraction towards Randy. But he was a hopeless romantic. As long as I remained available, his heart continued to invest.

13

MY PREROGATIVE

The line at Studio 9 was nearly a block long. Deemed the best dance club in Orange County, it attracted singles not only from its location just off PCH in Newport Beach but from surrounding cities and beyond.

"Wait here," she instructed.

I stood there at the end of the line and watched her walk towards the entrance to chat with the doorman until she disappeared in the distance. A few minutes elapsed when I noticed a figure standing out from the line. She was signaling for someone to come, animated, using her entire body to wave her arm. I wasn't sure if it was her at first, until I realized that, yes, it was Lori with her big blonde hair, long brown leather jacket, and high heels. We got in without paying any cover charge, and of course she scored free drinks all night long. I wondered about all those other girls who were waiting for hours in line. None, including myself, had the confidence or the swagger that Lori had to stroll right up and get an easy in. This was the way Lori got things done.

My story of Lori began at my first day job in SoCal. Unfortunately, even Top 40 bands don't earn enough money to pay the rent. Two months after moving to California, I landed a job as a receptionist at a sunglass-manufacturing company called Urban Perspective. Within six months, I was promoted and became secretary to the marketing manager. And Lori would eventually become the Marketing Assistant.

To this day, she remains the most fascinating person I would ever come to know.

14

THEY DON'T KNOW

nitially, I reported to Brendan Knight, who temporarily headed Marketing while the company was in search of a permanent marketing manager. Brendan, V.P. of Operations, was attractive and laid-back. I felt comfortable being around him from the first week, almost as if I had known him in a past life. But his supervision was temporary, and I was disappointed when he was replaced three months later by a new hire, Jay Lorenzo.

Jay, a single guy in his early thirties, wore a three-piece suit with a starched white shirt every day. His dark hair was meticulously combed straight back with no part, not a strand out of place. He had a perfectly trimmed mustache, which he carefully combed using a setting gel and a tiny comb specifically designed to groom mustaches. He was the type that could not walk past a mirror without checking himself out. Jay identified himself with the popular 1970s actor, Tom Selleck, but Jay didn't have Selleck's classical facial features. Jay's facial features were rounded, and Jay didn't have Selleck's chiseled body either. Jay's body was…well, slightly more rounded.

On Jay's second day on the job, I offered to get him a cup of coffee. The lounge was located on the opposite end of the building from the Marketing Department and was a bit of a walk. Since I was going to get myself a cup of coffee, I thought it considerate to get him one too.

"I'd love some." Jay beamed. "I like mine blonde and sweet—just like I like my women."

"Okay," I replied, awkwardly.

As charismatic as he tried to be, Jay had his bad days and took his frustrations out on me. But in the weeks and months to follow, he would experience a roller coaster ride of very few good days and many bad days, and my job would become far more intriguing than I could have ever imagined.

One morning as I walked past the front conference room, I noticed Jay conducting an interview with a cute blonde. He had this twinkle in his eye and an encouraging smile. He had informed me, a week prior, that he would be hiring a Marketing Assistant. The moment I saw her I knew she had the job. *Baby, you're hired,* I thought to myself, extracting the words right out of Jay's brain.

15

GYPSY

A few days prior to Lori's employment, Jay informed me that his assistant would start on Monday, spewing out her credentials, making it seem as though she was the bomb. He raved about how privileged we were to have her on board and what a great contribution she would be. And in case I was feeling slightly deficient, he offered a few encouraging words. "You'll be like a big sister to her, and working with her will be a learning experience for you both." The message I got was that she was free-range, grass-fed prime rib, and I was industrial ground beef.

Jay, pleased, to say the least, to have her on board, had big plans with Lori, business or otherwise. The great thing about Lori, from my perspective, was that Jay was in a good mood and on his best behavior every day. Yes, this was a happy time for Jay. He had a cute blonde Marketing Assistant with big brown eyes like Britney Spears, and a studious Amer-Asian secretary like Maggie Q. But there was so much about Lori that Jay didn't know. And it got good, *really good.*

From the get-go, Jay put forth great effort towards getting on Lori's good side, starting each day with his bright smile and his canned wit-washed rhetoric. He took her to lunch every day that first week and held private meetings with her, so he could impress her with his vocabulary. I knew he was doing this, because he had done the same thing with me. But ironically, something unexpected happened—Lori took an interest in me.

I was shy, diligent, and kept to myself. But Lori's desk was adjacent to mine, and she took advantage of the times when Jay was in a meeting to chat with me. She always greeted me with a sweet smile, sometimes accompanied by a compliment. "I love your patent leather shoes. I just moved here from San Francisco. What's the night life like out here?"

"I don't go clubbing that much," I replied.

"Really?"

"Well, actually, I do go to clubs, but I'm typically on stage performing."

"What?!" Intrigued, her eyes widened and she became visibly inflated with wonder.

"I'm in a band." I always felt uncomfortable with that statement, because without ever seeing me perform, I assumed a person would rate me as a *wannabe* as opposed to *the real deal.* And saying *I'm in a band* seemed immature, like something you'd say in high school. So I would always elaborate. "I'm in an original rock band. I play guitar, sing lead, and write songs."

Lori beamed with excitement. "No way! I would love to see you play!" And from that moment on, her focus was on me, and she poured on the charm. Only two weeks after Lori was employed, she and I started going out to lunch every day. She wanted me to hang out with her after work, and on the weekends, she seduced me with enticing invitations. "My boyfriend has a big sailboat. Why don't you come stay with me this weekend and go sailing?" Not only was she persuasive, she was beautiful, inside and out, and she won me over quickly, as she did with every person she met. But Lori had a secret she was never able to keep for long.

While Lori was a radiant and magnetic person, she lived her life with foolish abandon, ignoring all boundaries. She climbed the ladder, got hired, and reaped a fair ration of privileges by exploiting her charm, good looks, and at times sexuality which was the complete opposite of me. I had always achieved everything the hard way, taking the long, virtuous route. It was my mantra: honesty, integrity, and perseverance. In contrast, Lori's philosophy was if you want something, your only obstacle *is* your virtue. Rules were meant to be broken, and shortcuts were meant to be taken.

But with all of Lori's chips stacked high, there were flaws—flaws far too serious to ignore. Lori had addictions, and she was in denial about her extreme lifestyle and its self-destructiveness.

Jay became envious of my relationship with Lori. It wasn't supposed to turn out this way. He once tried to weasel his way in to our nighttime outings. "Where are you two girls going this weekend? Dancing? I love to dance." But Lori and I were evasive, and Jay couldn't find a way in. Finally, poor Jay just gave up.

Lori had been on her best behavior the first few weeks of her employment at Urban Perspective, because when it came to the nightlife, she was a level ten, while I was a mere level four. I could only handle two nights a week, but she was compelled to go out every night. These weeknight episodes had a direct impact on her performance at work. Jay would soon come to realize that his dream-girl Marketing Assistant was turning out to be a nightmare.

On a manic Monday, Jay asked me to go through the files and re-file anything Lori had misfiled. Incapable of multitasking, she could only be given one simple task at a time, and that task would take most of her day. She also had difficulty sorting out the steps to execute a project. She found herself diving headfirst into a project only to find an important element was forgotten early on resulting in a substantial financial flush. Eventually, she was routed to other areas of the office where she might be useful. She was temporarily placed in another department while a clerk was on maternity leave, but Lori was unable to get the numbers to balance on a spreadsheet. After several attempts, she invariably brought the spreadsheet to me to help her. Though I had made several attempts to train her, she was incorrigible. As time passed, without even attempting, she'd bring the spreadsheet directly to me with her puppy eyes and a sweet smile. "Can you do this for me?"

I accepted the spreadsheet without a word and without resentment. I knew she'd take care of all my wants and needs on our next night out.

Jay's meticulous nature made him cringe when he found Lori's scribbling on several file folders. Unable to discern the words, he discreetly asked me to read through the files and figure out what labels should go on the folders, then type new labels and switch them out. As the weeks passed, I received more of Lori's work, and so did Jay. It didn't take long before it became apparent to Lori that I was following her tracks, cleaning up after her, and so she confronted me, and I fessed up. "Sorry, Jay asked me to do it."

She was humiliated and resented Jay for increasing my workload, "My handwritten labels were fine! He's so fucking anal!"

The tables had turned in just two months, and Jay began to realize that he had been duped from the beginning. He became increasingly frustrated and embarrassed. I, on the other hand was a generator. I could handle the extra workload and basked in the daily juxtaposition of Lori and Jay.

In the weeks to follow, Lori's behavior spiraled out of control. She frequently called in sick because of her evening escapades. Other times she arrived at work late, wearing the same outfit she wore the night before and smelling like it too. She would walk to her desk around 8:15 a.m. to make an appearance for Jay; then she disappeared and spent another thirty minutes in the bathroom reapplying makeup—a new coat over the old one.

After lunch on the Friday before Memorial Day, Jay pulled Lori into his office to admonish her behavior and lack of work ethic, when suddenly her fun-loving demeanor took a 180-degree turn. Defensive and irate, she fired back. "My boyfriend is a lawyer, and I have my rights!" But her boyfriend wasn't a lawyer. He was a drug dealer—specifically cocaine and ecstasy—and Jay knew better than to fall for Lori's hollow threats. Naturally, the relationship between Jay and Lori turned cold henceforth. But one incident, in particular, pushed Jay's tolerance over the edge.

For two and a half days in July, Brendan sent me to an off-site training seminar to learn how to use a software program called Desktop Publishing. Jay, while sitting in his office, heard some murmuring and discovered Lori, under her desk, talking to people who were not there, obviously on some hallucinogenic drug. Jay escorted her back to the lounge and had her lie on the couch.

When I returned to work later in the afternoon, Jay asked me to drive her home. Shortly thereafter, Lori was terminated, and Jay and I took the workload. Since I had been doing her job anyway, it really had no impact on me.

16

DETACHABLE PENIS

"What's shakin'?" Randy asked the members of Crystal Image who sat together having lunch in the school cafeteria. The students at Huntington Beach High School came from predominantly well-to-do families. Randy, however, didn't fall into this category. He lived in a modest rental home and yearned to find his niche during his Junior year. He had saved up enough money to purchase a Fender Stratocaster and spent hours upon hours duplicating lead solos from the greats, including Eddie Van Halen, Randy Rhoads, and Jeff Beck. While the members of Crystal Image knew Randy played guitar, they had no clue just how advanced Randy had become.

"You guys going to enter The Battle of The Bands?" Randy asked.

Rick eyed Randy with a smirk.

Lead singer, Paul Cummings, responded, "Thinking about it."

"Cool," Randy replied, nodding his head several times over.

There was an awkward silence as Randy continued with his nodding. "Okay, look forward to it. Catch you later." Randy departed.

"Okay, look forward to it. Catch you later." Rick mimicked Randy, pulling his lower jaw in. Randy had an overbite, not quite as severe as the late Freddie Mercury, but pretty close. A couple members of Crystal Image laughed. Not so much as supporting Rick's cruelty but more so at the ridiculous look of Rick's contorted face.

"Dude," Paul whispered, "I think he heard you. Come on, don't make fun of him. He could be a really good guitarist. And Carl is leaving the band soon."

"He's a dork," Rick scoffed. "He probably sucks."

Randy was within earshot of Rick. And it hurt.

Over the years, Rick had grown to respect Randy as a musician, but on occasion, Rick would say something in jest behind Randy's back. Because Rick was the band clown, some of us blew it off while others laughed it off.

Months passed as I played numerous gigs with Crystal Image. After gigs, we hit the parties, usually hosted by one of our following. It was at these parties that Rick had an interesting idiosyncrasy of exposing himself, a ritual that I never witnessed, because I was either in another part of the house or chatting with someone in the same room and simply failed to notice. At some random point during the party, Rick would pull out his junk and let it hang for a few minutes while playing a game of pool or standing around the kitchen island. He would carry on and converse as though everything was normal. One day his penis got photographed and ended up on the refrigerator at Melanie's (a friend of the band). Everyone teased him about the size of it, and Rick never exposed himself again. It was the end of an era.

Rick, for the most part, was a good-natured guy, who smiled equally with his eyes as he did with his mouth. He always got hammered at parties and for some reason felt the urge to pick me up. He'd squat, wrap his arms around my hips, and lift me. My response was to squeal. But last time he did it, he dropped me. I stumbled back, and I fell flat on my back and banged my head which caused slight head spasms.

"What the fuck, Rick!" "Dude, don't ever do that again!" The other band members got pissed and berated him. I had to forgive him, because he looked utterly remorseful, like a guilty dog who got caught tearing up his master's most expensive shoes.

During my one-on-one songwriting sessions with Randy, he'd make comments about Rick. "Rick's not the brightest bulb in the pack," or, "Rick fell out of the clueless tree and hit every branch on the way down." But Rick was a genius at creating portmanteaus. He invented *fugly* and *vidiot,* using the terms two decades before they became common. And he was the first person I have ever heard call the hand lotion known as Jergens, *Jerkins.* "Every guy should have a bottle of Jerkins on his bedside table," he exclaimed.

As entertaining as Rick was, there was an initial concern that I had about him: his mustache, which he refused to part with. So I confided with Randy. "Can someone talk to Rick about his mustache? We're a rock band, not firemen. Mustaches are dated. It's the '80s now. Mustaches are long gone."

"I think he has a scar," Randy said.

"What do you mean? Like, right underneath his mustache? Is it that obvious?"

"Yeah, I think he has a hair lip."

"Oh... I suppose, since Rick's hair is long, he doesn't *really* look like a fireman." I decided to drop it. I would have to live with a drummer who looked more like the bassist for Spinal Tap, only a bit stockier.

Rick got booted out of his parents' home the first summer after I joined the band, for reasons unbeknownst to me. Rick couldn't afford to rent an apartment, so he slept in our rehearsal studio located on the second floor of a tiny run-down strip-mall in Huntington Beach on the corner of Adams and Beach

Boulevard. Occasionally, he asked one of us if we could let him use our shower. Then other times, he would take what he called a "whore bath" in the bathroom down the hall from our studio.

Late one evening just after booking a gig at The Hot Spot, Randy and I decided to go to the studio to visit Rick and smoke some weed. But when we arrived, Rick was passed out on the floor, covered with a blanket. He was snoring, so Randy and I decided not to wake him. We didn't realize Rick was naked until he rolled over onto his belly, exposing his bare bottom. Randy and I were stoned, and we doubled up in laughter at the sight of him. I got up and pulled a cigarette out of Rick's pack.

"What are you doing?" Randy asked because he knew I didn't smoke.

I tiptoed over and inserted the cigarette in Rick's crack; it stood straight up, nice and secure. Randy and I chuckled ourselves to tears. Rick didn't budge, and so I went one step further and drew eyes on one of his cheeks with a Sharpie, which gave us another bout of muffled laughter. Rick never found out about the violation, and Randy and I agreed to take the secret to our graves.

17

DATE WITH A KNIGHT

Brendan Knight took a special interest in me, sending me to training seminars every three to four months to continue my education in desktop publishing. I was never sure, in the beginning, why he chose me over Lori to attend these classes, but he obviously made the right decision, judging by the way things panned out. I eventually came to realize that Brendan was keenly intuitive on a super-human level.

With the creativity of desktop publishing, I was beginning to enjoy my day job. We eliminated some of the time-consuming manual processes, as well as the need to hire certain outside services. Eventually, a temp was hired part-time to handle the clerical work. Brendan upgraded my computer and software on a regular basis. When my second upgraded computer was installed, I could sense a tinge of envy from Jay when he looked over my shoulder and marveled at the new ad I had created in Adobe Illustrator.

Seven years older than me and a luminary at the company, Brendan might seem intimidating if you were to read his credentials on paper, but his personality was in complete contrast. Shortly after Lori was terminated, he informed me that he was taking me out to lunch on Secretaries Day. "Hey, you *were* my secretary for three months." We went to a nice, upscale French restaurant and ended up having a long conversation about the whole Lori ordeal. When we returned to the office, we were both cracking up. I had asked him his opinion about something—something he hated— and I knew he hated it the moment I saw his expression, but he didn't want to come out and say it. Brendan's expression was so telltale, I burst out laughing, and he joined in.

"Don't worry. You don't have to say it. Your face says it all." I chuckled.

"You're good with reading body language."

"No, you're just bad at disguising body language," I teased.

Before Brendan walked away, he said, "I enjoyed lunch today. We have to do this more often."

Jay, who was eavesdropping, confirmed his suspicions that Brendan had taken a shine to me.

18

PRETTY FLY

ori didn't take getting fired very well. She, of course, had put all the blame on Jay as though she had done nothing wrong. During her exit interview, she railed on Jay, and it got ugly.

In the next few months, Jay's behavior towards me turned warm, especially when a group of co-workers went to see my band perform at Madame Wong's with my glasses off and my hair down. The transformation, as Jay put it, was as metamorphic as caterpillar to butterfly. (The caterpillars I grew up with in Georgia were cute and fuzzy, so I didn't take that part as an insult.) In the weeks and months to follow, Jay began to depend on me for everything, and he tried to apologize in a roundabout way by explaining that Lori had lied to him during her interview.

"Don't worry Jay," I said, "we're cool."

A few months after Lori's departure, Jay asked me if he could get me a cup of coffee.

"Yes, please, I like mine black and strong, just like I like my men."

He looked at me with a crooked smile and left to fetch the coffee. Jay turned out to be not so bad in the end, and I ended up singing at his wedding one year later.

19

FIGHT FOR YOUR RIGHT

Every Thursday, like clockwork, I could count on a call from Lori to plan our weekend. She'd given up trying to get me to go out during the week. Unlike Lori, I knew my limitations.

Lori would show up at my gigs when she could find transportation. Her driver's license had been revoked, and she was dubbed by the state of California a "habitual traffic offender", which consequentially cost her some jail time. She had managed to accumulate a stack of tickets when she lived in San Francisco and never paid the fines. Then one day, the authorities caught up with her and hauled her off to a women's correctional center, where she peeled garlic, played billiards, and picked up cigarette smoking. Since her release, she had to depend on friends or the bus for transportation. Between her incarceration, a trip to Florida to visit her parents, and my weekend gigs, neither of us could find time to get together. Two months had elapsed before we could finally find an opening in our schedules, so I made plans to spend the entire weekend with her.

Newport Beach, sometimes referred to as Zooport Beach, was Party Central. Lori lived on 34th Street, just one block away from the boardwalk. It was the ideal neighborhood for her, since she was unable to drive. All she had to do was walk out her front door, and nearly every other neighbor was a party friend or a prospective one. Some were young professionals. Some were still in college. They mingled at the beach, on the corner, in one house, then the next. Orange County high school students would also flock here during the summer. They were all here for the same reason, to meet people and to be a part of the action.

I arrived at her apartment late Saturday morning. She greeted me at the door with mascara under her eyes, hair scrambled, and a big smile on her face. "Dude!" Her top was a super cropped T-shirt. Below, instead of underwear, she wore a one-piece swimsuit. The shoulder straps stuck out from her waistline and the bottom had ruffles across the rear. They reminded me of the type of underwear a toddler girl would wear over her diapers. It was a strange combination which did not concern her in the least. I surmised that she ran out of clean underwear, so she used the one-piece as a substitute. Had the T-shirt been a long one, she would have worn no underwear at all.

Two male roommates were watching football on TV when Lori reached up to get a mug from the kitchen cabinet. Her breasts popped out from under her top, and her roommates were on the ready to cop a peek.

She poured me a cup of coffee before we settled in her room, which was in a state of disarray. A crooked picture hung on the wall that matched a crooked lampshade. Draped on the lampshade was a pair of mangled pantyhose. Clothes were thrown all over the place. Her bed was a mattress on the floor with no sheets, just a blanket and a pillow.

She got dressed, and since it was nearing 1:00 p.m. she proceeded to make me boiled shrimp, when the phone rang. "Hi! My best friend is here, and I'm making her boiled shrimp. She's beautiful and plays in a band."

I could tell she wanted to make this day really special for me and making boiled shrimp was a big deal for her. She had gone out the night before to purchase them. This prior planning, though trivial for most people, would have taken a concerted effort on her part. I was touched. She over-boiled the shrimp, and they were presented warm, curled up tight, with a hard, rubbery texture. She was oblivious to the culinary faux pas.

"Shrimp with cocktail sauce is my favorite," I complimented.

Her entire face beamed with pride and joy.

Later, we walked on the beach, and she took my hand. She could sense my awkwardness towards her physical affection. Dejected, she let go. And I immediately felt ashamed. Lori, in many ways, was quite different from me. She had the open arms and heart to make friends quickly. In some cases, I had been leery of some of the shady characters she associated with. I, in contrast, took months, maybe years before I could decide if a person was worthy of my complete trust. I was organized. She was chaotic. Although there were many polar character traits between us, we enjoyed being together. I suppose we had a mild fascination towards each other. She made me feel special, and hanging with Lori was always an adventure. She was the yin to my yang. Lori would always remind me to bring my acoustic guitar to perform at local neighborhood parties, and I loved doing it. I achieved instant small-scale fame, love, and respect from her friends and neighbors. Since I never had a sister and had no other girlfriends in California, I cherished our friendship.

20

BEEN CAUGHT STEALING

On a sun-drenched Saturday afternoon, Lori's eighteen-year-old boyfriend, Michael, and his friend, Ryan, met us at the beach. Later, we walked to The Pelican's Nest, located at the end of Pier 46. I ordered a bottle of chardonnay, a bucket of steamed clams, and some sourdough bread to share. At the end of our snack, we sat and waited for the waitress for a good fifteen minutes to take my credit card. After twenty minutes, with still no waitress, I decided to go to the bathroom located by the front door. Lori stood outside the bathroom waiting for me when I exited. "Come with me!" She pulled me out the front door, and the second we made it down the stairs, she interlocked her fingers with mine. "Run!" She took off like a bullet, nearly yanking my arm out of the socket, and I ran with her. And we kept running and running. Several yards behind us, Michael and Ryan had no choice but to follow our lead. When we reached the pier front, we blended into the crowd, panting. Michael, vexed over the runner, expressed his disapproval. "That's bad karma!"

Truth be told, I felt guilty about the runner even though it had been one of the most exhilarating experiences I could ever recall.

Later that evening, Lori and I made plans to go to Hollywood to see Cory's band perform at The Roxy on Sunset. Her high success rate for scoring freebees during our night on the town was based upon being single, so she had no intention of having Michael tag along. As it turned out, Michael's disgruntlement over the runner made a perfect opportunity for Lori to dismiss him.

Dinner that evening was a bottle of chardonnay, brie cheese, a sliced Asian pear, and a French baguette. As I applied my makeup in the bathroom, Lori walked in to pee. Because there was no toilet paper, she wiped her crotch on the towel hanging from the towel bar.

"Uhhh, remind me to bring my own towel next time I visit," I said.

"Oh…that's my towel," she explained. "No one else uses it. I'll go get a clean one." But there was only one bathroom in the apartment, and only one towel on the bar. If I hadn't said anything, it would have remained there for the next unassuming victim to use on his face or hands. She took the towel off the bar, threw it in the tub, and hung a clean towel in its place.

Decked out in tall black boots and spandex mini-skirts, Lori completed her outfit with a satin and lace corset and an acid-washed denim bolero jacket. I wore a similar ensemble with a Sergeant Pepper jacket. Long loose curly perms were ubiquitous of the times, and we wore ours big. We drove to L.A. with music blaring Guns N' Roses, Missing Persons, and Oingo Boingo.

The Roxy was packed, but we managed to score a corner table closest to Cory's side of the stage. Lori zeroed in on Cory and was star struck. In spandex leggings, Cory paraded the stage shirtless. His long hair draped over defined pecks and ripped abs. He owned it. He scanned the audience, sensuously. His band mates sported big smiles whenever they made eye contact with each other as if they had a band secret. Sometimes they laughed like they were having the time of their lives. They were brothers in arms on top of the world. Maybe their secret was that they knew they would each have two beautiful girls on each arm after the show.

Lori's eyes were intense, glued to my brother. Later in the evening she said, "I love your brother. He's a male version of you."

I had managed to straighten my slouch for the most part, but didn't quite carry Cory's confident arch. We continued to watch him as he worked the crowd, dominating his bass guitar.

After the concert, we drove back to Orange County to a party in Newport Beach, just one block from Lori's apartment, and around 3:00 a.m. Mr. Sandman cast his spell, and a multitude of yawns escaped my mouth. I wasn't sure how Lori remained so alert at this hour, but I suspected that sometime during the evening she had partaken in crystal meth. I never understood the appeal of meth. Sure, it kept you awake so you could party your brains out, but for me, the crash, when you finally came down from all those toxins, seemed unbearably sickening and depressing. I couldn't rationalize trading a wild all-nighter for almost 48 hours of lethargy and shame. Lori had never pressured me to use it with her, and she exercised utmost discretion to hide it from me, knowing that I'd judge her.

As time passed, Lori began to recognize the polar differences between us. "For a girl in a band, you're very conservative." "You're so tidy." "You made this hollandaise sauce from scratch?" "You actually sewed that corset? It looks so tailored." Because Lori had to spend every waking minute of her life in the company of another, she was incapable of accomplishing a solitary endeavor like refinishing a vintage chair or cooking an elegant meal.

As I fumbled for my car keys, Lori insisted that I stay with her. "No way in hell! I can't let you drive home in this condition. You'll fall asleep on the road, silly girl. Now you listen to me Margee

McGuire, almighty-fucking-stubborn-rock-goddess, you need to rest your ass here at my place and *go to sleep*." She knew I had issues with her bare mattress, so she found a clean beach towel to place on the bed. I collapsed, and within seconds I fell asleep. But between consciousness and sleep, I had a recollection of her gently removing my boots and singing "Superstar" by The Carpenters, and it sounded sweet.

21

WALK THIS WAY

I opened my eyes to unfamiliar surroundings. Gradually, I realized where I was. My foggy brain could vaguely recall Lori and me performing on the bar playing air guitars to Crazy Train while everyone danced and cheered us on. She played lead guitar and I played bass—big smiles on every face.

I decided to quietly sneak away, but Lori woke up, and as usual she pleaded with me to stay.

"But I don't want to wear these dirty clothes," I contested.

"You can borrow mine. Come on, I'll make you breakfast. There's a volleyball tournament today in Huntington Beach. It'll be fun. What else have you got to do?"

Inevitably, her art of persuasion would squash my better judgment, so we picked out clothes, and I got dressed.

"How do you like your eggs?" she asked.

"Sunny side up with the whites fully cooked and the yolk barely cooked. If you cook the eggs on low heat and put a lid over the pan for a couple of minutes while it's frying, it comes out perfectly. But you have to keep checking it, because you don't want the yolk to harden, and it gets hard fast if you don't pay attention." I got my eggs with the yolk broken and cooked hard. They also had a tiny bit of a crunch as a piece of eggshell ended up in them. Lori explained that if I make a sandwich out of the eggs with the buttered toast, I wouldn't notice the hardened yolk. "What's your brother doing today?" she asked.

I shrugged because I was chewing my egg sandwich, which actually did taste pretty good.

"Let's call him and see if he wants to hang out with us."

The AVP Pro volleyball tournament at Huntington Beach was a good call. Little did we know we were seeing rising stars in action including Misty May, Kerri Walsh, and Karch Kiraly. Afterward, Lori, Cory, Randy, and I, enjoyed beers and shrimp tacos on Main Street. As the sun drew near the horizon and our shadows became blissfully buzzed giants on the boulevard, we drifted back to the van to drive Lori back to her apartment. She stepped out of the van, waved goodbye, and as she walked to her stairs, Cory called out to her from the passenger window, "Hey, Lori."

She turned around.

"Come here. Don't just walk away like that," Cory chided in a mock-serious tone.

Lori approached the passenger window where Cory was sitting.

"Come here," Cory repeated in a softer tone. The second Lori encroached his bubble, he grabbed her head with one hand and planted a heavy-duty kiss on her lips. She was flabbergasted, and I have to admit, so were Randy and I.

During my following visit to see Lori, she went on a rampage about Cory. "Can you believe how he just grabbed me and kissed me like that? The audacity! I mean...(scoff)... What makes him think that he could do that? We hardly even know each other. I'll tell you one thing, homey don't play that."

I thought about the girl who kissed me all those years ago in Augusta from the mental institution, wanting to tell Lori *it could have been much worse.*

But no more than an hour later, Lori asked me to call Cory to see if he wanted to hang out with us again.

Lori had her sights set on Cory, and she managed to have her way with him at least one time that I knew of. The summer of 1988, Cory was living with California girlfriend number three, Devon, so Cory's encounters with Lori were brief. However, one Saturday while Devon was away for the weekend on a business trip, Lori paid Cory a visit at their apartment in Huntington Beach. When Cory's girlfriend returned, she discovered that a valuable piece of jewelry had gone missing—a jade cross necklace set in gold stamped lacework. A gold medallion sat nestled in the center crest of the cross. I remembered the necklace well, because I admired it. I had never seen anything like it, and I knew that Devon cherished the piece very much. It had been a gift given to her by her late father, who had brought it back from a business trip in Japan when Devon was ten. Devon was heartbroken. Cory had no way of knowing for sure that Lori stole the necklace, but he was highly suspicious due to the timing. The day before Lori showed up, the necklace was in its usual place on a crystal platter on Devon's vanity. The day after Lori's visit, the necklace was gone. As a consequence, Cory decided to disassociate himself from Lori. Since there was no real proof that Lori took the necklace, I couldn't pass judgment. But a red flag came up.

22

WHAT I AM

Lori videotaped one of our performances at The Golden Bear. As we watched, she fantasized. "I want to work with your band when you make it. You'll need someone to assist you with all sorts of things like your wardrobe, ordering your food for backstage... I can do anything... You'll need me, Margee." I pretended to go along with her ideas, careful not to crush her ego or fantasies.

Fall in SoCal could be windy or a tad chilly, but most of the time vividly sunny and slightly cool in the shade. I visited Lori again the following Sunday afternoon. It was another perfect California day.

Over the years, I had kept a collection of songs in a large red notebook. Most of the songs were never recorded or even made it to stage, because I felt they lacked integrity. I had progressed beyond four chord songs. But Lori appreciated the simple and repetitive nature of my early material. "How about you sing lead, and I'll sing harmony," I suggested.

"Seriously?" She was thrilled—beaming like a five-year-old. Lori didn't have the best voice, but as time passed, it got better and stronger with encouragement, coaching, and practice. She had a tendency to go flat at the very end of a phrase, but I resigned to accept it as personal and stylistic. In every other aspect, she imitated my voice, even the slightest nuances and intonations, identically.

I took it a step further and taught her to play some easy chords on the guitar. If she learned the chords, then I could play some lead solos. To my surprise, she actually practiced during her alone time and showed improvement the following weekend. I was also impressed to see that she had acquired a beautiful new guitar. "Is that a Martin?" I asked.

"My new boyfriend. He works for Martin."

"You're kidding. He just gave you that guitar? Think you can get me one?"

"Yeah... I'll probably have to give him a blowjob though," she responded nonchalantly as she strummed a chord.

"Oh... Never mind. I really don't need another acoustic guitar."

Some weekends we spent a good four hours singing and playing songs. Uncharacteristically, Lori began to ask questions about the business side of music. "Hey Margee, what do you do to protect your songs?"

"What do you mean?"

"I'd be afraid of someone stealing your songs. They're really good. And I really like the older songs. You guys should play them."

"Well, I do copyright any song that we record and the songs we perform on stage. But these old songs? I don't really worry about them. No one is ever going to hear them. It doesn't really matter."

"How do you copyright a song?"

I shrugged and explained. "It's just paperwork with a cassette tape of the songs, and then you mail them to the Library of Congress in D.C."

Bemused, Lori gazed at me and nodded.

23

DIGGING YOUR SCENE

Brendan and I continued to have a platonic relationship. I intended to keep my promise that I made to myself: success first, romance after. So I kept my distance from Brendan for the most part. But he and I developed a special bond over time, engaging in deep conversations over lunch, and we discovered that we shared the same interests as well as philosophical and political views. During lunch at an upscale Japanese restaurant, we arrived at the topic of raising children. "If I have kids, I'll want them to be with me," I expressed. "I don't judge other mothers who put their children in daycare. It's just *my* personal choice. I know I won't be able to leave them. Even when my cat was a kitten, I refused to go to Vegas for one night with some friends, because I didn't want to leave him. I felt guilty for going to work all day and leaving him in the house by himself. If I feel this way about a cat, you can only imagine the torment I would go through leaving my baby every day with a nanny who I don't really know."

But the possibility that I may never have children had crossed my mind. Time would eventually run out. I was twenty-seven and had no way of knowing how long it would take to land a record deal.

Brendan supported my stand on raising children. "My mother was career driven—always working. I love her, but I don't feel a close bond towards her," he confided.

We fell silent as I folded my paper chopstick case into a chopstick prop.

"When we worked together in Marketing, I looked in your desk drawer for a paper clip and noticed you separate the big paper clips from the small ones, and you color-code the files by sales region. I would bet that you have dividers in your bathroom vanity drawer separating all your various types of combs and makeup, and you probably have your lipsticks divided by color too."

I let go a hearty laugh. It took a few moments to gain composure. "Oh my God. Am I that bad? For some odd reason, I have one drawer packed full of contact lens cases. I must have seventy-five of them, but I just don't feel like they're the type of thing to throw out. By nature, I'm an anti-hoarder, so when I look in that drawer, I always go back and forth through my mind. Do I keep them? Or do I throw them away?"

"Really? You know I never have enough of those contact lens cases."

"Well there we go! I'll give you some of mine."

"Deal."

We shared a childlike chuckle.

The following day I mailed Brendan an interoffice envelope cram-packed with every contact lens case I had, excluding one. I imagined his puzzled expression just prior to opening the envelope, as well as his expression upon finding sixty-eight contact lens cases, and I giggled. Two days later, I received an anonymous inter-office envelope filled with hundreds of pennies. It weighed about fifteen pounds.

Careful not to lead Brendan on, I used several methods of diversion. There were rehearsals, gigs on the weekend, and dates with Sanjoy, a special friend who worked in the Design Department.

His brilliance combined with his creativity placed Sanjoy on another level above the average human. I noticed him for the first time at the company Christmas party where he entered the ballroom on the Queen Mary, dancing flamboyantly. *What are the odds?* I thought to myself, *a queen, dancing to "Dancing Queen" on the Queen Mary.*

I fell in love with him at first sight. And we clicked just as fast as he could snap his fingers in the air. One night at Santana's, Sanjoy decided to "come out of the closet". We were sipping Margaritas during happy hour after work, when suddenly he became very serious. "Margee, I have to tell you something." After some hesitation, he proclaimed, "I'm gay."

Bemused that he would think his sexual orientation was a secret, I replied, "I know, honey."

Astonished, Sanjoy asked, "How did you know?"

"Oh, let me see... You love to go shopping with me to pick out stage clothes. You skip when you're happy. You wear colorful silk scarves. You own five pairs of designer glasses that you change according to your outfits. Rather than walk, you have more of a sashay. Should I go on? My gaydar went off the first day I met you."

Sanjoy burst out in his typical high-pitched laughter. And with his feigned British accent he blurted, "Oh, sweetie, I just adore you. You simply can't imagine how much I adore you."

And I responded with an equally masterful British accent, "Likewise, darling. Come now, hugs."

24

WE CLOSE OUR EYES

Problems began to surface with Crystal Image. Rick started to flake out, missing rehearsals and arriving late at gigs. Our bassist, Mike, expressed his misgivings about Rick's drumming on more than one occasion. "A drummer and bassist should work together as a team, but Rick's in his own world."

I also had reservations about Rick's drumming which revolved around meter issues—coming out of a fill a tad too late or starting a song too fast so we were stuck playing the song at top speed in its entirety. We pressured Rick to play with a click track, but this made him miserable. He began to miss more rehearsals. Finally, we decided that we had no choice but to let him go. I felt really bad about it. Since Randy led the band, he was given the task to tell him. I was grateful I didn't have this job, even more so when I spoke with Randy afterwards.

"How did it go?" I asked.

"It was worst thing I ever had to do. His face got all red, his eyes welled up, and then he just walked out."

Deep down, Randy and the rest of us knew that replacing Rick would be the only way to reach the next level. Two months later, we found a replacement.

A first-place rudimental champion in high school, Greg Safa had perfect meter and a perpetual sense of humor. He not only filled the role as drummer, but on a more mature level, he also filled Rick's shoes as band comic. Greg was also inherently diplomatic. One of his greatest virtues was the gift of communicating issues in such a tactful way you could accept them without offense. He became the band mediator. When tempers began to flair, he was on-the-ready to smooth everything out, easing any type of tension between members. He was also good at pumping up a deflated ego and came to my rescue on several occasions. When he auditioned, he passed Mike's scrutiny with flying colors.

But solving the problem of our rhythm section was just one issue among several that were beginning to emerge. We continued to submit promo packages to major and independent record labels, but we weren't getting any bites. Although Randy was an exceptional guitarist, and his song writing skills were up to par, there was nothing unique about his songs. They were too mainstream rock. Between learning cover songs, Randy's originals, rehearsals, and gigs, we had only gotten around to learning two of my songs. In order to maintain congruence within the band, I introduced songs that fell within the genre of Randy's style of songwriting. But our songs lacked the edge and originality necessary to stand out from all the other bands. We sounded a tad too much like Journey with a female singer.

Randy idolized Journey. But record companies didn't need another Journey. Plus, anthem rock, in 1989, was becoming passé. Music was changing by leaps and bounds. In a band meeting, I expressed my feelings fluidly and my desire to make some changes that would take us to the next level. "Guys, I think we need new songs—songs that are truly original, different, updated. Our image could use a makeover too. And since I'm on a roll here, a kick-ass stage presence—one that will seize the audience and never let them go. If we're going to be called original, then let's be it. Let's develop a new, original sound. We need to be unique…one or two steps *beyond t*he current trend with our sound, our image, and our stage presence."

Guns N' Roses had already taken L.A. by storm when they came on the scene with unfettered hair, bare chests, tattooed arms, and snakeskin boots. The whole glam craze vanished overnight, and of course every young band in L.A. followed in Guns N' Roses' footsteps. I didn't want to climb on to that band wagon. On the horizon, a new movement was taking place in America on both the East and West coasts with rock music. Rap was no longer reserved for the black artists, in general. There were new, hard-energy groups like Rage Against the Machine, Beastie Boys, and the Red Hot Chili Peppers. They rapped and they rocked hard. Up north, Seattle was spawning a new garage raw, hard rock sound called grunge.

With a new palette and a blank canvas, Randy and I began creating songs that would breathe new life in the band. We focused on vocal and musical hooks. We integrated dynamic contrasts, shifting gears now and then and let the guitars drop completely out in certain parts on a couple of songs. I convinced Randy to stop writing love songs. And rather than follow the trend of depressing lyrics—typical of grunge—we began writing lyrics with a positive upswing.

But there was a traditional element that seemed to be lost in rock music during those days which I really missed: great vocal harmonies. Although Randy was already a great backup singer, I had to teach Mike how to sing, and this was a challenge because Mike didn't have the confidence.

Unexpectedly, Derek, our keyboard player, informed us that he would be leaving the band in June, relocating to Northern

California to accompany his father in his flourishing tile business. The news was a blessing in disguise from my point of view. Derek straight out laid down the law that he would never sing. His departure would open up the opportunity to hire a keyboard player who could contribute backup vocals to the band.

But finding a replacement was difficult. Weeks dragged into months. Randy failed to renew our ad in the Recycler, which irritated me. Expecting a dry spell, I was surprised when I answered the phone, and it was a keyboard player.

In October 1989, Trevor English, a spunky Australian with short, bed-head hair, strolled in for an audition. Not only did he have the look, he was highly technical and owned innovative gear, including three keyboards and a Macintosh computer. He embellished our songs with cool patches, layers, and hooks, *and* he could sing backup.

25

KISS THEM FOR ME

"What! You mean completely bald?" Greg refuted.

"All I'm saying is if a guy is going bald anyway, or if he has a major receding hairline, he may as well shave it all off."

Excluding Trevor, the other band members were slipping behind the times. When a rock band's image falls behind the times, they end up looking like contemporary country. Look at any popular new country band, and typically you will see what rock bands used to look like, minus the cowboy hat, in some cases.

One way to be fashion forward was to subscribe to *Vogue*. But most straight guys won't do that. We were nearing the year 1990, and the original Crystal Image needed a serious makeover as they clung to the late 70s/early 80s. They panicked when I suggested cutting their hair. "Come on guys...trends change and evolve, much faster than you can imagine. The trend for hair is getting shorter. Shaved heads, for the first time in history, are cool."

Trevor was a huge asset to my campaign as the other band members took notice when the girls were drawn to him like bears to honey. I recommended several image options, which they found hard to swallow: edgy designer suits, short bed-head hair, eye-lined eyes... But the suits were out of the question and out of their budget. I needed a concept they could grasp. So I searched through *Vogue* magazine and stumbled upon a perfect photo shoot with guys and girls hanging out in London.

"The look is cool but a tad gay," Mike expressed.

"But wouldn't you agree that gay guys tend to be fashion forward? They know what's sexy, and they aren't afraid to be cutting edge. Besides, remember the glam phase? Guys were wearing lipstick, eyeliner, eye shadow, *blush*... The women loved it. Right? What about Jimi Hendrix, Prince, Mick Jagger—fast forward—The Chili Peppers...Look, I just think it's important for our band to make an audio *and* visual impression."

Going out on a limb, Greg bought fitted dark grey Dickies with a flat front that sagged just a tad. "I still think these look weird. I'm going to miss my pleated acid-washed jeans." he chided.

"One day you will see that weird is good. That's what you want. Be weird. That's what rock stars do. We have the artistic license." But I still needed to broach the subject of his mullet. Finally, one day I just came out with it. "Dude, you have to cut your mullet off. It's not the '80s anymore."

"Girl, what are you talking about? This isn't a mullet."

"Okay, well, whatever you call that little bit that's growing down the back of your neck. Cut that bit shorter. Actually, get rid of it completely, 'cause it's giving me an achy-breaky heart."

"What? The ladies dig my hair."

"The country ladies, yes, *they* do."

"Trev," Greg appealed, "be honest. Does this look like a mullet?"

Trevor answered Greg's question with a question. "Does a one-legged duck swim in circles?"

"I'm going to have to take you down, bitch," Greg chided. "You guys are just jealous 'cause I'm too sexy for my face."

"Yeah, that's it," Trevor responded. "I'm getting a ten-inch right now just looking at you."

Randy, on the other hand, had always been supportive with my suggestions. He also bought dark grey Dickies and accessorized with a studded belt and a long silver pocket chain.

"Fitted T-shirts, Randy," I explained. "Baggy T-shirts and those baggy saggy pants are on their way out. You guys are in great shape. Sell it. Keep in mind, ahead of the trend, setting the trend, not following the trend."

Both Randy and Greg bought Doc Martens for footwear and consigned a gifted, up-and-coming street artist to design fitted, silk-screened T-shirts.

Mike scored a flirtatious, sheer, short-sleeve black button-down shirt that he found at a designer boutique on Melrose. He paired it with pin-striped black pants that he scored from the Salvation Army thrift shop in Santa Ana and had them altered to a slim silhouette. He spent a small fortune on a sleek pair of designer shoes and dyed his dark hair platinum.

Everyone's hair, except Randy's, went short. Trevor chose a long-sleeve, button-down black and blue striped shirt from his wardrobe and paired it with electric blue velvet pants.

As for me, I have always been into contrasts—contrasts in textures and contrasts between masculine and feminine. I wore knee-high, black cherry Doc Marten boots paired with a short, silk slip-dress in crimson. The slip had a short hemline and was just tight enough to show the curves underneath. Over the slip I wore a sheer, crimson low-cut tunic that dropped below the silk hemline. To top it off, Sanjoy recommended a well-known hair designer in L.A. who cut twelve inches of my hair and transformed it into an edgy, chin-length layered bob with shattered ends. I colored my hair mahogany, which looked great under stage lights but conservative enough at the office. I kept my face out of the sun and wore porcelain ivory foundation, no lip color, but dramatic eye makeup in the classic Joan Jett fashion. An old black guitar strap embellished with faux fox fur draped across my shoulders and down the base of my guitar.

With the new band members and a fresh new image, we scheduled an appointment for a photo shoot. I hired a photographer, who specialized in fine art photography. This set Randy and me back a $1,000, but it was worth it. The photographs were extraordinary.

The photographer recommended that we bring two outfits. We decided on a winter theme for the second image. I sewed a full-length crushed taffeta skirt in crimson. The skirt was formal, like the bottom half of a spectacular wedding gown, and it hung on the hips, revealing a bit of waistline skin. On top, I wore a fitted, red leather jacket, embellished with buckles, snaps, and zippers. From elbow to palm, the jacket flaunted mahogany red faux fur with a faux fur collar that wrapped around the shoulders.

In black and grey tones, the guys sported black leather jackets, pea coats, or knee length wool blazers with scarves, along with black boots loaded with silver hardware. The photo, taken with a green screen background, was captured as though we were walking towards the photographer. With Photoshop, I manipulated the photograph and dropped our image in the midst of a soft, surreal winter snowfall, walking down a desolate street lined with bare, snow-frosted trees on both sides. The collection of new photos blew our old band photo out of the water. The guys were beginning to realize how far behind the times they had let themselves go. Much hard-earned money and effort went into producing these images, but we finally had a band photo that would stand out above all the rest.

26

YOU SHOOK ME ALL NIGHT LONG

In 1982, Paul Cummings was the lead singer for Crystal Image. But Crystal Image played only a handful of gigs and never really got established, so there was no real need to continue with the name. Since we had started anew in every other aspect—members, songs, image—I figured it was the perfect time to change our band name. And though I had never mentioned it before, I wasn't partial to the name Crystal Image. It seemed ordinary to me, plain, safe. It would have been a great name for a window cleaning company. But for a band, we needed something avant-garde and better fit for a band fronted by a female lead vocalist. So we tossed around dozens of ideas for names, but deciding on a new name for the band was no easy task.

Mike was hooked on the name Green Banjo Dog. But Green Banjo Dog, in my opinion, was a terrible name for a band fronted by a female singer. Relentless in his efforts to persuade us, it was to my relief when he finally gave up the fight.

It was Taco Tuesday at Santana's. We were having a few beers, and Mike was feeling a good buzz after our third pitcher. On stage, a great cover band called Switched On was performing classic hard rock from the '70s. During their break, they joined us. Mike asked them what they thought of the band name, Green Banjo Dog.

"Is she in the band?" the drummer asked, nodding towards me.

"Yes," Mike replied.

"Well she ain't no dog!"

Everyone had a good laugh, and nothing else was ever mentioned about it again.

Choosing a band name is typically an ordeal. It's like five parents, with different personalities, settling on one name for a baby.

Quite often, Greg had to dart out of rehearsals as soon they ended, so he was never around afterwards to give any input or participate in discussions about band names.

"Look Greg," I said, "we really need to settle on a name, and we should all be together to discuss it."

"I tell you what," Greg offered, "I gotta get going, so why don't you guys come up with three names, and let's have a band meeting to decide on the name once and for all."

When Greg left the studio, I had an idea. "Hey guys, let's play a joke on Greg."

27

DO YOU REALIZE??

The following Friday night, I invited the band over to my condo to discuss band names.

Greg was sitting directly across from me as I read each one. "Okay, let's talk about the first name, Bunnies N' Toes."

One by one, the band members left the table and began pacing behind Greg, so they were no longer within his line of sight. Two were bent over holding their mouths. Mike was silently shushing them with a vertical finger over his lips, rocking back and forth smiling with all his teeth, and all his efforts seemed to only encourage the opposite. They were dying of laughter in complete silence. Surprisingly, Greg didn't notice.

Exercising a formidable amount of self-control, I diverted my eyes back to the list.

Mike gained his composure and started to talk about the name. Pacing in Greg's peripheral, forearm across his chest and the other hand gently pinching his chin like Steve Jobs, he began to verbalize, tentatively, his fabricated thoughts. "What's good about that name is that it's sort of like Guns N' Roses, except you take the two-syllable word and place it first, and you take the one-syllable word and place it last."

Trying his best to be diplomatic, Greg responded cautiously. "Well...okay...it isn't *really* like Guns N' Roses, is it? I mean... (sigh)...Guns N' Roses has a real coolness to it, but Bunnies N' Toes? I don't know... I don't know."

Greg was shaking his head when Trevor interjected. "Dude, it *is* like Guns N' Roses if you think about it. You have the feminine and masculine contrast in both. Guns and Toes are manly sort of words, yeah? And then Roses and Bunnies are feminine. I reckon it's a pretty cool name."

I concluded, "I like it too. It has a nice flow, and if you keep saying it over and over, it grows on you. Bunnies N' Toes... Bunnies N' Toes... Yes, it's a good one for sure."

Mike and Trevor nodded several times to confirm.

Greg, with his brow scrunched and lips pursed in serious contemplation, was nodding ever so slowly completely falling for our hoax.

At the time, we didn't realize there existed a psychedelic alternative band from Oklahoma called The Flaming Lips, and it was by sheer coincidence that we came up with the same name. The musical compositions of The Flaming Lips are unique and sophisticated, yet easy to absorb. Taking advantage of technology, they use a discriminating choice of effects and a tasteful array of instrumental layers. Their lyrics are often entertaining and thought provoking. The Flaming Lips are esteemed for their elaborate live performances featuring puppets, balloons, and a giant hand, to name a few. But what I remember most about The Flaming Lips in concert is that the lead singer walked around stage in a human size bubble, which I thought was pretty cool.

However, there was one curiosity about the name of the band. I don't know if there was an alternate meaning to the word *flaming* in Oklahoma, but specific to California, the term *flamer* is slang for a male homosexual, and if a guy is referred to as flaming, it means he's gay. *Not that there's anything wrong with that.* However, it just so happened that Greg was a tad homophobic.

"Anyway," I continued, "next one: The Flaming Lips."

Greg's face began to flush, and he drew in a long breath followed by a slow exhale.

I started off by saying, point blank, "I think it's an ultra-cool name."

Trevor and Randy agreed.

"Definitely a possibility," Mike added.

"Really, guys?" Greg refuted. "What's the last name?"

I read the last name on the list. "Okay, I think this one is my favorite: Nigel's Closet."

The guys, straining to suppress their laughter, had to avoid being in Greg's view altogether, or he would know we were toying with him.

Randy, who was able to compose himself, came to our aid. "I came up with Nigel's Closet. It has a real coolness to it. It's got that..." Randy raised his palms to emphasize his next two words, "mystery factor. You sort of wonder, like what's in Nigel's closet? Who is this chap Nigel?"

"What?" Greg blurts.

"Uh huh," I said, "and if you keep saying it over and over it starts to grow on you." I repeated the name with a British accent. I pretended to be an emcee introducing the band. "Good evening, Daytona Beach. Please welcome NIGEL'S CLOSET!"

With Greg's face contorted in bafflement, the rest of the guys were bent over restraining their laughter. On the brink of his tolerance, Greg reproached me. "Girl, what is it with you saying it over and over? I mean, if you say Anal Emerson over and over, you might start to like it too, but it doesn't mean it's a good name."

Unable to hold it in any longer, I started to laugh uncontrollably screening my face with my fingers.

Greg was eyeing me suspiciously, when it dawned on him. "Are you guys fucking with me?" He quickly swung around, and no one could hold it in any longer, bursting out hysterically. Relieved, Greg joined in, laughing himself to tears. "Thank God."

The meeting lasted another hour tossing around the real names, but we still could not settle on any of them.

28

ROSES GROW

"Hey Randy, what do think about using Scarlet for the band name? Pair it up with another word."

I made a concerted effort to conceal my southern accent, but once in a while it came out, especially if I drank too much or became frustrated about something. So Randy had given me the nickname, Scarlet. "What do think about, Scarlet Divine?" I suggested.

"We can't use Scarlet Divine. It's the name of a porn star."

"Okay," I laughed, "that's out."

After a forty-minute brainstorm, we finally came up with Scarlet White.

"I like it!" Randy exclaimed. "It rolls off the tongue like Concrete Blonde. It's strong, but has a feminine quality."

Concrete Blonde was an alternative band fronted by an L.A. girl named Johnette Napolitano. Johnette was a badass bassist with a mesmerizing voice exemplified in her hit single, "Joey".

"It is similar to Concrete Blonde," I concurred. "Both Concrete Blonde and Scarlet White contain three syllables. They're both broken up by two words with an accent placed on the last word. Concrete Blonde is a color, and so is Scarlet White if you stretch your imagination just a bit."

We continued to analyze the name and discovered that red represented excitement, speed, strength, energy, desire, and passion, while white represented peace and simplicity, which characterized our new music well. We rocked hard, yet we had some songs that grooved and other songs that were mood driven.

To sell this idea and the name to the rest of the band, I decided to present it to them in a couple of logo formats. At the following band meeting, the name Scarlet White was voted in, unanimously.

29

HIT

The main stage at Bogarts was open without curtains. I was back stage with my new cordless mic, while the boys had already started the intro to our newest song, "Language of Love", a song that was loaded with energy and rocked hard. Seconds before my vocals came in, I appeared on stage and performed this first song without a guitar. It was my chance to just be a front for the band. It felt almost liberating to be able to spread my arms wide and focus only on vocals and moves. It was a perfect opening. And we kept the audience transfixed for the entire show as it grew in numbers. People were coming up front from all areas of the club. They packed together around the stage, smiling, dancing...

At the rehearsal prior to our gig at Bogarts, we had a discussion about stage presence. "There can be no dead time," I stressed. "We're on stage for only ten songs. As soon as we are introduced, we slam into the first song with high octane energy; when one song ends, another song will start.

"There's going to be a short break in the middle of the set. That's when I talk to the audience." It's important to talk to the audience, even if it's just a few words. They like that personal touch, that inside story to what the next song is about or even just to say how happy we are to be there. "It's not only about each individual song being tight but how the songs flow from one to the next. Just before the last song, I'll thank the audience, and we finish off with '006'." I wanted the band to understand that the most important factor apart from great songs, was our stage presence and treating the performance as if we were a major headliner act. "We need to give the people what they paid for and more. If we are going to 'make it' we are going to have to 'fake it'. In other words, make an impression as if we already have a stage manager and all the trimmings that signed bands have."

Greg had already made it clear that we had to control our levels. Loud bands were immature bands. And they cut their own throats, because the sound engineer cannot get a good mix when a band is cranked up too loud, making it impossible to hear vocals above the instruments. The audience doesn't really like loud bands. What the audience likes is a great mix. What the audience likes is hearing the vocals.

"You know what else would be good?" I added. "If you guys jumped up—right on those upbeat accents on 'Too Good'." So we did. It was as simple as any ZZ Top move, and just like ZZ Top, the audience ate it up. It was those little extras that would pay off every time we took the stage.

The entire band got on board. Ideas on how to improve our act flowed from each member. And it became a natural evolution for the boys to become more invested in their stage image, stepping out far beyond their old comfort zone. As the wheel of creativity spun, Scarlet White began to reach greater heights.

The money I shoveled out for my image and band photo shoot set me back. I had to buy cheap shampoo, cut coupons, and eat peanut butter and lettuce sandwiches for nearly a year to stay afloat. But those photos put us into the larger venues like The Coach House, The House of Blues, The Galaxy Theater, and The Troubadour. The winter photograph was posted around Hollywood Boulevard and Sunset Strip. We placed them side-by-side in columns and rows. Looking at the photos, you would think the band members stepped out of a limo or Learjet. You would have never imagined that the girl in the band drove an old Mitsubishi pick-up, shivered in the winter, and melted in the summer, because she couldn't afford to pay an electric bill.

30

JUST LIKE HEAVEN

Returning home from work, I parked my car on the curb and found Trevor asleep in his car, so I woke him up and invited him in. His hair was a mess, and he had a 5:00 shadow. When he stepped out of his car, he yawned and stretched, pushing his chest out. He was tall, slim, and defined, and his back was always perfectly straight even when he was tired. He smiled at me with a twinkle in his eye, perked up quickly, and began teasing me about my conservative work clothes. Then he carried on with his naughty secretary fantasies. "She's walking towards me, unbuttoning her blouse. She takes off her glasses and pulls her ponytail down. She pushes me back against the photocopier..."

Trevor was also the youngest member of the band, eight years younger than me. Outspoken and profoundly creative, he was an interesting character with contrary traits. He was meticulous and obsessive-compulsive about being in control and doing things a certain way. To offset his internal tension, he went overboard—drank himself from buzzed to oblivion during his off time. When alcohol entered Trevor's system, he seemed to lose all inhibitions, shooting moons out car windows and stripping naked at parties to settle into a hot tub. On one occasion, he took a running leap off a roof, au naturel, into a pool some thirty-five feet below. For Trevor's sake, it was a blessing that Greg was a responsible drinker.

Greg, Trevor's wingman, was typically on hand to drive Trevor home from parties or clubs when Trevor got hammered. Greg's good sense of humor and quick wit hastened their initial bonding. During rehearsals, Greg bantered with Trevor. And so, it became the norm to see the pair hanging out together on the weekend when there were no gigs.

On a Thursday evening following work, Randy, Trevor, and I had scheduled a low-volume rehearsal to create integrated keyboard and guitar parts for a couple of new songs.

I had been alone in the condo for over thirteen months since my brother, Will, transferred to Japan for an exchange assignment to teach English to Japanese servicemen. So the condo living room was temporarily transformed into a nice little unplugged rehearsal studio.

Not wanting to drive all the way back home to Laguna Beach after his college classes in Irvine, Trevor came directly over to my place to hang out until Randy's arrival at 7:00 p.m.

Since Trevor was fairly new to the band, I hadn't quite gotten used to his sexist humor, although my experience with Darcy had taught me that the best way to handle these situations was to respond with a witty retort. But quick wit was a trait I had only admired in others, because I didn't have the gift. I seemed to come up with something clever a few seconds too late when the moment was lost. But I definitely felt impressed with myself the few times I could catch the ball and throw it right back. Abashed, I tried to conceal my true emotions. "Yes Trevor, you keep entertaining yourself with your special fantasies. I'll make sure they never come true, so you can keep this special fantasy forever."

"Well, you know, I have other fantasies too, heaps and heaps of them. It's perfectly okay if this one comes true."

Speechless, I shook my head and chortled.

We entered my condo. "Make yourself at home. The beer's in the frig."

"Okay, if you insist."

I left Trevor in the living room and went to my bedroom to change my clothes and to wash my face. A few minutes elapsed when I heard Trevor giggling.

"What's so funny?" I yelled.

He didn't respond, and the giggling continued.

A bookshelf, located in the living room, encased a collection of hardbacks and two photo albums from my childhood. When I returned to the living room, Trevor was holding one of the photo albums, chuckling. "Check it out." He flipped the album around to reveal a picture of me wearing a karate uniform in a low-profile guarding stance, taken when I was ten. My Dad insisted that I portray a ferocious look on my face. So I ended up with a ridiculous expression. Waggishly, Trevor posed to imitate the stance and facial expression. "I kill you!" he uttered with a gruff Japanese accent.

Annoyed, I tried to snatch the photo album out of Trevor's hands before he got to the next pictures, which were equally—if not more—embarrassing. When I was six, I impulsively shaved off one eyebrow playing with my dad's razor. My father thought it was cute, so he took a head shot photo of me with one bald eyebrow and an innocent toothless smile on my face. I grabbed for the album, but Trevor dodged me. He ran around the dining table. I rounded the table after him, and then he darted down the hall.

"Give it to me, Trevor!" I yelled. "You can't just go looking through my personal things."

I pursued him into my bedroom, but he quickly jumped on my bed face down with the book under his belly, both arms wrapped around it. "I just want to see it!"

"Not now. We need to work on the songs!"

"Okay, but after I see the rest of the pictures first. I won't laugh, I promise."

"That's a bunch of bull, and you know it, Trevor." I jumped on the bed, straddled him, and tauntingly whispered in his ear. "All right, so this is how you want to play? Fine. You are *so* going to regret this, because I've got you now. You ever heard of Chinese torture? Well guess what? Margee torture is worse. Let's see just how ticklish you are. This is going to be so much fun. How's this?" I poked his rib with one finger, and he twitched. "*Okaaayy*, a little ticklish are you?"

Alternating right to left, I poked his ribs side-to-side, and with each poke, Trevor twitched, squeaked, and began to pant heavily with dreaded anticipation.

"Get ready, Trev, 'cause I'm preparing for attack mode. Ready, set, now!" And I attack-tickled his ribs with gusto, showing no mercy.

"Stooooppp! Okay, you win! Stop!" Trevor screamed. "Here's the book... Bloody hell!"

Trevor was panting heavily. I allowed him to roll over so he could surrender the album, but he shoved it under the pillows and began to counter-attack tickle me. I tried to tickle him back while guarding my ribs, but it was difficult. We were both laughing and screaming hysterically. Though Trevor was bigger than me, I was putting up one hell of a fight until suddenly, he flipped me over, straddled me, restrained both my arms, and landed a kiss on me that was to be the most unforgettable kiss of my life.

Being the baby, and the only girl, I was protected by my three older brothers. They were my body guards. And they let it be known that any boy who dared to touch me would suffer the consequences. Boys knew better than to cross boundaries with Margee McGuire. Consequently, friendship status was as close as I could get with a boy, which is why I had always felt very comfortable around them—unthreatened—and boys seemed mutually comfortable around me.

So I became one of the boys. Paradoxically, my introversion flipped to extroversion when I was with the boys. I biked with them, I skateboarded with them, and I joked with them. I became a top-dog boy and could crack jokes and do imitations that would bend them over in laughter. But the thing I never did with boys was kiss them.

Trevor's kiss paralyzed me for a few seconds followed by hungry reciprocation. His lips gravitated down to my neck. I could only imagine that this was what a blast of opium would feel like entering my bloodstream. My heart was racing—my senses amplified. Here we were, heaving and panting, as if headed towards an explosive sexual climax. Twenty-eight years of virginity had made me lose my senses, and I was behaving like a wild animal.

Within ten seconds, I put it to an end. I shoved Trevor away and retreated to the kitchen. A few moments passed before he entered kitchen. I could sense his presence. "You *do* realize that if we don't take care of this, I'm going to have blue balls."

Oh my God, I thought. *Did he really just say that? Really?*

The doorbell rang.

"We'll talk about this later." Flushed and embarrassed, I went to answer the door.

When rehearsal ended, both Randy and Trevor continued to hang around as if one were waiting for the other to leave. I finally dismissed them both, claiming to have a headache. "I need to go to bed, guys. I'll see you on Tuesday."

But sleep escaped me. I tossed and turned in bed, and I couldn't get my mind off Trevor—how intoxicating his kiss had felt—and how pathetic I was. How was it possible that I could be a twenty-eight-year-old girl in a rock band and had never had sex? Was I that focused on a musical career to such an extreme that I had ignored other facets of life, such as love, passion, and romance? Feelings that meant so much to normal people. Did I allow myself to miss out on a magical experience with Trevor? But then I would have broken my first band rule, not to mention the risk of pregnancy. Although sex was something people did at the drop of a hat. All you needed was a condom. It really didn't have to mean something. Or did it? What if I just wanted to have sex with no commitment and no emotional attachment? What would be so wrong with that? If the woman was game, it could only be an ideal situation for the man. What single man wouldn't want sex with no strings attached?

I pondered the harsh reality that I had been cheating myself out of years of explosive physical pleasure. All those years lost that I would never recover. So I made a decision. Tomorrow morning I would take action and finally cross the bridge from girl to woman.

31

BRASS IN POCKET

arrived at work with intentions. I used a little more makeup than usual and spent more time on my hair. Brendan had given up asking me out on dates after I had turned him down twice. Once, he had tickets to an Angels game, and the second time he had asked me if I wanted to go see *Phantom of the Opera* at the Pantages. The last time I turned him down, I imagined his heart dropping down to the pit of his stomach, given by the dejected look on his face. Now, it could be that the tables would turn. I could be the rejected one, and there would be no plan B. For the first time, I fully understood the courage it took for a guy to ask a girl out on a date. Why would Brendan want me now, after I had turned him down twice? I also caught wind through Sanjoy that Brendan had started dating a woman he'd met on a group ski trip a few weeks ago, which further thwarted my courage. Unwilling to be afflicted by my anxiety the entire day, I jumped on my first opportunity. Brendan strolled into the lounge just as I was getting a cup of coffee. I greeted him cheerfully. "Good morning." We made some small talk about the weekend.

"Your hair looks pretty," he complimented.

Then out of the blue, I popped the question. "Hey Brendan, you know for the first time in I don't know how long, I'm free tonight. Do you want to go grab a bite to eat?"

Taken off guard, he responded with a blunt, "Oh."

"If you're busy, it's no big deal—"

"No, no. I… Can I get back to you this afternoon? I just have to rearrange some things."

Later that afternoon Brendan informed me that it was set, and rather than going out to dinner, he would prepare dinner at his place. Impressed, I raised my eyebrows and smiled.

32

ONE THING LEADS TO ANOTHER

"**I** want to know everything! Now don't leave out a single detail."

The following day after my date with Brendan, Sanjoy and I had made plans to see an art exhibit in L.A. During the drive, he was incessant with questions about my date with Brendan. As much as I tried to avoid the discussion, Sanjoy ignored any form of evasion and pressed on. "So what did he make for dinner?"

"Mahi mahi. It was really good. He made this delicious papaya salsa to go with it."

"Very nice!" Sanjoy responded in his silly French accent. "Continue. What else did Monsieur de le Knight prepare for mademoiselle?"

"A salad with champagne vinaigrette dressing."

"Ooh, la la. And did he make ze dessert?"

"Rum raisin ice cream. He remembered it was my favorite, and he had to drive to an ice cream shop in Costa Mesa to get it."

"Oh, how sweet!" Unabashed, Sanjoy continued to probe. His main objective was getting to the evening's climax. "So what else? What happened after ze dinner?"

"Sanjoy!" I blurted, shaking my head, hoping he'd give it up.

With a heavy sigh, he returned to his American accent. "Oh my. You're still a virgin, aren't you?"

The same day that Sanjoy opened up to me and told me he was gay, I shared with him that I was a virgin. Ironically, he did not reciprocate with the same sensitivity as I did regarding his disclosure. He reacted as though only an insane person would hang on to their virginity for so long, as I recall our conversation. "Sanjoy, I didn't go on about you being gay."

"It's queer, sweetie."

"I know. You've told me that before, but I don't like saying that word. It sounds offensive to me."

"Anyway," he replied, "being queer is a natural thing. But a virgin at your age is not. Look at you. You're a sexy girl. I don't know how you do it to be quite honest."

"I spend my time focusing on a future, not sleeping around like you."

"I can't help it that I'm such a hottie."

At the time, I made Sanjoy promise not to tell anyone that I was a virgin. I was embarrassed about it.

Sanjoy sat in my car in silence. Finally, he offered some consolation. "Oh, sweetie, it's all right. Your day will come."

Screw it, I thought. "Okay, you win. No, I'm no longer a virgin. Are you happy now? Is that what you want to hear?"

Sanjoy exploded with glee and clasped his hands together to his heart. "My baby girl is all grown up!"

All I could do was roll my eyes.

He then started singing Donna Summer's *"Bad Girls"*. Snapping his fingers and swaying in his seat, he continued to entertain himself.

I couldn't help but giggle as I gave him a playful push. "You're the bad girl! I don't know how I put up with you."

My evening with Brendan had been sublime. Our conversation flowed freely, and we laughed through dinner over two bottles of wine. Afterwards, I asked Brendan if he had any photos from his past, so he pulled out a box of pictures, and we browsed through them while he reminisced. I put my head on his shoulder, and he put his arm around me. We kissed with no ending… I could hear Mazzy Star in the background, and I faded into him.

In the morning, Brendan asked me if I wanted to spend the day together at Laguna Beach, but I told him I had already made plans with Sanjoy. Overcome with curiosity, Brendan asked, "Margee, was I your first?"

With my fingertips to my forehead, I screened my flushed face and confessed. "I'm such a dork."

"The last thing you are is a dork." With a hint of a smile, Brendan hugged me tightly and kissed my hand.

33

THE REAL SLIM SHADY

Since Lori had relocated to L.A., I had not seen her in eight months. Following the exhibit, Sanjoy and I met up with her for a late lunch. Though Sanjoy had only met Lori briefly while she and I worked side-by-side with Jay Lorenzo, he had developed a fondness and fascination with Lori from stories I had shared with him about her.

Over lunch, Lori produced some interesting news about her current undertakings in L.A. "I'm singing lead and playing guitar in a band now! We're called Tunnel Love. My new boyfriend, Dean, is managing us. Oh, and my new stage name is Lourdes Love."

For some reason, I found the news unsettling and felt a tinge of envy. Throughout our friendship, Lori had expressed her ambitions to be an artist, a dancer, and an actress. I had always supported her dreams and aspirations, but she was never able to summon the drive towards making those dreams a reality. I pretended to be happy and congratulated her.

Admittedly, Los Angeles suited Lori. Later in the evening, she took us to two underground nightclubs. The first venue was dark with several rooms that flowed from one to the next. At one point in history, it had been a large family dwelling until it was converted into this insanely cool L.A. nightclub. The main room, called The Cave, was located downstairs in the basement where artificial stalactites hung from the ceiling. The Pandoras, an all-girl rock band, was performing. Each band member had big long hair, and each girl wore a different color lingerie-esque outfit. Their audience stood packed in around the stage. I felt as if nothing could top The Cave until Lori took us to a dive bar located two streets off Hollywood Boulevard.

Situated down a narrow alley, we descended a set of stairs to enter this hole-in-the-wall with a total of six long tables—the quintessential biker bar. We took a seat at a table when a slim shady character sat next to me. In my peripheral, I could see his hands were adorned with silver rings on every finger. Lori leaned over and whispered in my ear, "The guy sitting next to you is in Guns N' Roses." My heartbeat turned into thump. Appetite for Destruction had just been released, and it was rapidly becoming the number one album in the country. I must have waited ten minutes when finally, I mustered up the courage and said, "I like your rings."

He wore aviator style sunglasses with a newsboy cap. Dark hair swept out from under his cap surrounding his face down to his shoulders. To my surprise, he began to tell me a story about every ring.

"So what do you do to pay the rent?" I asked.

"I'm in a band called Guns N' Roses."

"I've heard of you guys. Heavy metal, right?"

"No, we're not heavy metal at all. A lot of people think we're heavy metal, but we're hard rock."

"Don't you guys have a song in that new Clint Eastwood movie?"

"Yeah, 'Welcome to the Jungle'."

"I like that song. Did you get to meet Clint Eastwood?"

"I did. He's a nice guy. I shook his hand and said, 'Clint Eastwood, make my day.'"

I laughed out loud. In contrast to his biker, bad-boy persona, Izzy Stradlin was charming and innocently sweet. We closed the bar down, and the four of us, Lori, Sanjoy, Izzy, and I, walked to Denny's for breakfast. While we were seated, someone walked up to our table to talk to Izzy, followed by another person, then another, and another. Izzy appeared uneasy with the escalating attention, and within seconds, he slipped out and disappeared into the night.

Lori and Sanjoy hit it off, and she invited us to a party in Beverly Hills the following weekend hosted by a wealthy executive at Pixar. Though I wasn't able to attend, Sanjoy pounced on the opportunity.

34

BAND ON THE RUN

Mike's sister, Melissa, lived in the San Antonio suburbs. She and Mike were very close, and so it was her wish to have her brother's band perform at her wedding in late March. Though we had become a full-time original band, we decided to work in a few covers for the party. To supplement, Melissa had also hired a D.J. to work the later hours, as well as a jazz quartet to perform earlier while guests were mingling, dining, and in-between toasts.

Melissa's fiancé was the heir to an oil tycoon, so financing this grand party was of little concern to them. Our flight and accommodations were paid for, all-inclusive for the entire weekend. We were put on a Friday morning flight out of Orange County Airport the day before the wedding.

I arrived early at the airport, checked in, and was waiting at the gate when I spotted Greg and Trevor. We greeted each other, and Greg left to get a cup of coffee. Trevor and I made some small talk, when I decided to take the opportunity to discuss the incident that took place in my bedroom two weeks prior. "Look,

Trevor, I don't want you to get the wrong idea. What happened at my place was a mistake and can never happen again."

"Okay," Trevor replied. "That means you're going to have to control yourself when you're around me."

"What?" I scoffed. "What are you talking about? *You* kissed me."

Trevor shook his head. "Excuse me young lady, but *you* jumped on top of me. *You* straddled me. *You* whispered in my ear—blew your warm breath in my ear. You had your hands all over me."

"Are you serious? Hands all over? I was tickling you! I did not have my hands all over you."

"You were teasing me."

I laughed, sardonically, at such an outrageous accusation. "Teasing you? Oh my God. That's ludicrous. I wasn't teasing you, Trevor—"

"You know what I can't figure out? You want me. *I'm* wondering what's holding you back. What are you afraid of? Why don't you let me teach you a thing or two?"

"Are you kidding me? I'm almost twenty-nine years old, and you're twenty-one. What could *you* possibly teach *me*?"

"I used to date an older woman."

"Okay, first of all, I'm not a cradle snatcher. Second, I don't date guys in the band. Third, I'm not interested."

"Uh huh," Trevor responded. "First of all, you shouldn't judge a person by their chronological age. Secondly, you seemed to like the little sample I gave you. Third, if you'd have given it a chance, it would have just gotten better and better. You would have experienced a big bang in the end."

I began to a laugh nervously and repeated, "A big bang."

"Well...actually, more like a massive eruption that goes on and on."

"Ohhh, a massive eruption," I said sarcastically.

"Yeah, that's right—that goes on and on. Maybe you'll get

your chance one day."

The conversation was getting so ridiculous all I could do was laugh. In the distance, I could see Greg, now joined with Randy and Mike approaching. "Just forget it then, okay? This conversation is over."

"I can forget about it, but the question is can you forget about it?"

We arrived in San Antonio and checked in to our hotel. We were all in a cheerful mood, fully relishing our mini vacation. Mike left early to meet with his family to attend his sister's dinner rehearsal later in the evening, so around 6:00 p.m., the four of us, Randy, Trevor, Greg, and I, decided to have some Texas BBQ and drinks. The concierge referred us to a place with a good reputation for BBQ and a full bar.

Built in the 1950s, the establishment was a large, classic red barn that had been converted into a two-story restaurant with a mechanical bull in the center lower level. On the weekend, many of the locals gathered here to go line dancing on the second level. We were seated at a circular booth and began to partake in an evening of hijinks and folly. I lost count of how many pitchers of Texas Ice Tea had been ordered, but by 10:00 p.m., Trevor was inebriated. By 11:00, he was hammered.

Two miles away on Highway 313, an ostrich farm stretched across six acres that we had passed on the way to the hotel. Jokingly, Greg made a comment that Trevor would be streaking through the ostrich farm before the night ended, and the band broke out in laughter. Though Greg had not meant it seriously, Trevor, in his state of mind, needed no coaxing. He made a bet, and one by one, we all agreed to pay Trevor $25 each if he ran butt naked through ostrich territory.

When we arrived at the farm, it was nearing midnight. We drove the perimeter in search of an area to park that would be concealed from the freeway. The moon was full, so it wasn't difficult to discern the white fence that surrounded the property.

Making our way down a short dirt road tucked between tall underbrush, we drove a few yards, turned the headlights off, and parked. Accompanied by a choir of crickets, we trampled through the underbrush and made our way to the fence where we agreed that the lone tree approximately fifty yards away would be an acceptable marker for Trevor to run to and back. Trevor jumped the fence and undressed.

By the year 1999, a ten-foot, double chain-link fence would encompass Turner Farm. But the fence Trevor had to scale in 1991 was only five-foot high and made of wood. He climbed over the fence, stripped, and handed his clothes to Greg. As my eyes traveled the landscape of Trevor's body, my gaze was interrupted when Trevor's eyes met mine. He smiled discretely and winked. I quickly diverted my eyes.

Our intrepid keyboard player began sprinting towards the tree, and we were all overcome with fits of giggles at the sight of him. As Trevor drew near the tree, I had to do a double take. In the distance, I spotted an ostrich jaunting in Trevor's direction. Trevor rounded the tree, jumped up, and gave a click to his heels; then he began skipping and flapping his arms like wings. The others were cracking up. And I would have joined them had I not become aware of the approaching creature. My eyes darted back and forth from the ostrich to Trevor as the ostrich advanced faster than I would have ever imagined, and within seconds, he became visible to the others. "Trevor! Ruunnnnn!" I screamed, and the others joined in. Trevor turned his head to discover, to his fright, the giant bird making a beeline in his direction. Trevor bolted, shifting straight into fourth gear. He reminded me of a cartoon character running so fast his legs were moving in front of his body. But the bird was gaining, and I wasn't sure if Trevor was going to make it. Suddenly, just a mere ten yards from the fence, Trevor tripped and fell flat on his face. And to our horror, the giant bird trampled him followed by multiple stomps on Trevor's back. Trevor began to holler out obscenities as the bird continued to dance, "Fuuuck! Bloody hell!!!!"

Instinctively, the three of us jumped the fence without caution, and I doubt that any of us had any idea how we were going to rescue Trevor. I was holding a mini flashlight that I had taken from my purse. "Play dead, Trevor." I stood halfway between the creature and the fence and shone the light in its eyes. It stunned the bird instantly, relieving Trevor from the trampling. Slowly, the creature began moving in the direction of the light, as I walked backwards towards the fence.

Greg hoisted Trevor off the ground, and they scampered to safety.

Because we had caused such a disturbance, we headed straight back to the car. In the distance, we could hear the faint sound of a siren. Fear had replaced our joy and imposed upon us an intense sense of urgency.

Had our evening's venture ended at this moment, this night would have gone down in history as a lesson well learned. But fate was not merciful to our folly, and our troubles had only just begun. Floodlights blinded us once we reached the dirt road, and like the ostrich, we were stunned. From a loud speaker, we were ordered to lie down on the ground. I felt extreme dread, especially for Trevor, who was hurt and lying belly down on the dirt butt naked. The officers approached us, and suddenly I felt sick. For some odd reason, I began conjuring up perverted images from the film *Deliverance*. I tried to banish these horrific images from my mind, but they just kept popping back like a bad song. With a Texan accent, one of the officers spoke. "Boy, what the *hell* are you doin' naked?"

"I made a bet. I was going to streak through the farm, but I chickened out. I changed my mind, and we were just going back to the car."

"Do y'all know you're on private property?"

"No sir," Trevor replied.

We were read the Miranda rights, handcuffed, and driven to the police station for detainment and further interrogation. It turned out to be a grueling evening. Around 7:00 a.m., a policeman released us, stating that the owner of the ostrich farm did not want to press charges. But before he let us walk, we were escorted to the Chief of Police.

Haggardly, we filed into his office and stood before a brawny, grey-haired man with a stern, chiseled face. Holding our file, he peered over his reading glasses and eyeballed us one by one. "Which one of y'all is Trevor English?"

Trevor raised a heavy hand.

The officer then removed his glasses. "I just want y'all to know that this young man is damn lucky." Focusing his attention on Trevor, he sat back and began his lecture. "Young man, I really don't know whether you actually crossed the fence and encroached upon the ostrich territory, but it's mating season and the male ostrich is extremely aggressive and territorial this time of year. Son, you have no idea."

Of course, Trevor did have an idea. He had firsthand experience.

The officer continued. "An ostrich has talons. I'm talkin' talons like a velociraptor. Those talons can slice you open with one fell swipe, and *kill—you—dead*." The officer then addressed all of us. "The reason Mr. Turner is not pressing charges is because he's attending Miss Hatfield's weddin' today. I understand y'all are supposed to perform at the reception, so we're going to let this affair slide and pretend it never happened. Now, I don't want any more trouble from you people. *Is that clear?*"

"Yes, sir," we mumbled.

The chief shook his head at Trevor. "Boy, you had better go see a doctor. You look like hell."

And Trevor felt like hell. He had paid dearly for his foolhardiness. The ostrich attack had left him with two broken ribs, and the fall, due to a pothole in the ground, had sprained his ankle. He had an agonizing hangover, and to add salt to his wounds, the brush that he ran naked through was poison ivy. Trevor remained stoic throughout our performance at Melissa's wedding. He didn't actually become aware of the poison ivy exposure until he returned home a day later, and it besieged every inch of his body.

35

THERE MUST BE
AN ANGEL

When we returned to Orange County, Trevor needed some time off. With his parents living in Australia, Trevor really had no one to reach out to, so I drove to Trevor's cottage at Laguna Beach to bring him some food and videos.

Small and barely furnished, Trevor's one-bedroom home was three blocks from the beach. The living room was furnished with a small sofa, a chair, and an old television. Three keyboards, a computer, a mountain bike, and a surfboard filled the remaining spaces in both the living and dining areas. The layout was similar to Jack and Ellie's, but Trevor's cottage was fairly new. The bathroom contained a beautiful antique claw-foot bathtub. I was curious how Trevor, a student, struggling musician, and part-time barista, could afford rent on a cottage at Laguna Beach, but came to the conclusion that his parents were most likely pitching in to help him.

With all his injuries, Trevor had done a good job keeping the place tidy. But he looked pathetic. After unpacking the groceries, I found him struggling to do laundry while holding one crutch. I took his arm and led him to a chair. "Why don't you just sit here and fold; I'll do the rest."

"I knew you cared."

"I'd do this for any of you guys."

"No, there's more there. I have a keen sense about these things. You like me more than the others. Oh, and by the way, watch out for Randy."

"What are you talking about?"

"I reckon he fancies you—always carrying your equipment for you—and the way he calls you Scarlet, his special pet name for you. It's annoying."

"He's harmless, Trevor. Besides, I've already had a talk with him about it. He knows where we stand."

"Sure. Whatever you say."

With a light heart, I came to accept Trevor's flirtatious nature and found myself looking forward to his company. I returned every day for the following two weeks to help him out and was amused by his enthusiasm to share his knowledge.

"What are you going to teach me today, Trevor?" I teased.

"I told you I could teach you something."

As the days passed, I continued to receive a heavy dose of laugh therapy. After a history lesson on the slave trade from Africa to America, I made a comment. "It's amazing how much information is stored in that messed-up head of yours. I'm calling you Clever Trevor from now on." At which point, I had to dodge an oncoming sock missile. I ducked and the sock landed in Trevor's beta fish bowl.

"Hey! You won a fish!" I exclaimed.

"Oh no! Quick, get it out. Sushi will get stressed out!"

I stomped my foot in laughter.

One evening, as we finished the dinner dishes, the subject of my photo album came up.

"I shaved off my eyebrow when I was six."

"Why would you do that?" Trevor asked.

"I was six. I didn't know what I was doing."

"Yeah, but you're looking at yourself in a mirror, right?"

"I was in a trance. I was mesmerized by seeing my eyebrow just vanish. I wasn't thinking about the future. It wasn't until I was done that I looked at myself and realized I screwed up majorly."

Trevor began to giggle gingerly.

"I don't know why my dad had to photograph me. I looked so stupid with one eyebrow. It might have been different if I were blonde. You know those pictures where you have to guess what's wrong with the picture? Well talk about obvious. You look at that picture and it's like—*bam*... And those wide unsuspecting eyes... that toothless smile... My father was exploiting my innocence by taking that photo."

Unaware of Trevor's agony, I continued to ramble. "He knew how ridiculous I looked. And I thought he was just taking a picture of me, because he loved his little baby girl... I should have shaved the other eyebrow off so both sides would match."

Trevor laughed with more intensity and whimpered, "Uhhhh, my ribs."

"Okay, I'll stop. Sorry."

"No. I mean...can I please see the photo? After my ribs heal?"

"Oh, all right." I sighed.

"Thanks. You know you're a real sweetheart."

"And don't you forget it."

"I won't. But don't you think you would have looked just as weird with no eyebrows at all?"

I pondered the question. "Then I could have just drawn them in with a makeup pencil."

Trevor, unable to contain himself, started laughing even though he was in pain.

I reconsidered my statement. "No. That wouldn't have looked right either. I would have looked like a damn circus freak." I busted out with laughter, imagining a six-year-old girl with self-penciled eyebrows.

It was hard to tell whether Trevor was crying or laughing. He moaned.

"Oh God, sorry, I'll leave soon. I'm nearly done here."

"No! Don't leave me! It's only 8:00. You stayed till nine last night. If you don't like those photographs, why do you keep them?"

"I can't throw them away. I'm afraid I might regret it down the road. If I keep them, they're safe with me. I have control over who sees them. This way, when my dad visits, he gets to see them and have a good laugh, and then the photos get put away. And no one else gets to laugh at my expense."

"Except me."

"Yes. Except you, Trevor."

I made arrangements for Greg and Mike to visit Trevor over the next two succeeding weeks. Trevor refused to have Randy drop by. He pouted and asked why I couldn't keep coming instead of the other guys. "What else do you have to do?"

"I do have a life, believe it or not."

"But what could be more fun than coming here and visiting me?"

"You're doing much better now. And you can call me any time."

Trevor had been getting around much better with his crutches and was able to do more on his own. He had also learned that by combining an antacid with an antihistamine, his rash cleared in two days.

On my last day at his place, I said my goodbyes to Trevor. "You'll recover less painfully without me making you laugh."

Oddly, Trevor surrendered a melancholy expression, an expression that seemed uncharacteristic for him.

"What? What is it, Trevor?"

He seemed intent on wanting to tell me something but hesitated. "Never mind. It's nothing."

I scrutinized him. "Okay, take care, my friend." Conscientious of his injured ribs, I kissed him on the cheek. As I turned to walk away, I caught a glimpse of his face, and he looked genuinely forlorn.

36

I'M NOT IN LOVE

Madame Wong's, located just outside L.A. in Santa Monica, was a large venue with three levels and three stages. Oingo Boingo, The Police, Guns N' Roses, to name a few, had headlined here during their rise to stardom. Tonight, we would be the headlining act, and seeing Scarlet White on the marquee felt surreal.

The basement level was closed to the public. It housed a large commercial kitchen of stainless steel shelves and appliances that the club did not utilize—a remnant of the days when Madame Wong's was a large restaurant. There were several rooms across the kitchen corridor for storage. Bands used these rooms as a dressing area and often gathered in and around these rooms following the show. Lori arrived to watch our concert and later met me downstairs by our dressing room.

During our performance, Lori zeroed in on Trevor. "I see you have a new keyboard player. He's cute. What's his name?"

"Trevor. Aren't you in a relationship with your band manager? I thought you two were serious. What was his name? Dean?"

"We're on again, off again. Currently, we're off. Is Trevor by himself tonight?"

"He's been seeing some girl recently." But it was a lie. Trevor didn't have a girlfriend. I don't know why I lied, but for some reason, I didn't want her to have him.

Over the years, during my evening escapades with Lori, I was okay with her taking the cream of the crop. On first impression, the gorgeous guys were attracted to her. And I never cared. But this time, it was different. I couldn't explain or understand my possessiveness towards Trevor.

As we turned the corridor to the open area just outside the dressing room, we could see Randy, Mike, and Greg sipping beers and chatting with some girls. Across the corridor in the kitchen area, several other bands, groupies, and friends were socializing, including Trevor. Lori strolled directly over to him, extended her hand, introduced herself, and began pouring on the charm. As always, she was confident she would score. "Hi, I'm Margee's best friend, Lourdes. I sing and play guitar in a band called Tunnel Love. You make a great addition to the band."

"Thank you. That's a lovely compliment coming from a fellow musician."

"I *love* your accent. Are you English?"

"Well, yes and no—better." Trevor was equally flirtatious, slightly coy. They smiled. She nudged him and looked him up and down. She stood close to him, giving him the green light big time.

I didn't like it. I wanted to warn Trevor about her. I wanted to tell him that she'd been with a hundred guys. But I couldn't. I'd sound jealous and stupid. Besides, I had a boyfriend. Why should I care? But I did. So when Lori went to the bathroom, I seized the opportunity. She would be returning soon, and the possibility of her and Trevor leaving together pinched a nerve. I took Trevor by the arm and pulled him aside. "Trevor, I hope you're not thinking about having sex with her."

Surprised, Trevor recoiled. "Margee, are you jealous?"

"Noooo, no, no..." I swished my hand and blew air through my lips. I shook my head side-to-side to show how preposterous it was to assume that I could ever be even remotely jealous. And in thirty seconds or less, I made my case. "Listen to me, Trevor. She was incarcerated last year. She sleeps around like nobody's business. My brother really believes she stole his girlfriend's necklace. She slept with my brother while his girlfriend was out of town." I lowered my voice. "*And*—" I checked my right and left for eavesdroppers. "She had genital lice two weeks ago. I just don't want you to do something you'll regret. Your penis just recovered from poison ivy. Do you really want to subject it to the crabs now? I'm just sayin'."

Trevor studied me. "Is this how you talk about a best friend?"

Shame devoured me. He could sense my contrite heart. I wore a pleading expression fused with guilt splattered all over my face. I shouldn't have trash-talked her like that. It was unconscionable. But I didn't lie completely. She *was* in jail last year. And she *did* acquire genital lice, albeit six months ago. But the necklace allegation was sheer desperation.

Trevor's facial expression transitioned from slight annoyance to revelation. Upon his epiphany, he put his beer down on the counter, slid both hands in his pockets, and stood so close to me I could smell his cologne—it was intoxicating. His body was nearly touching mine, as he carried an aura of dominance. The energy was vertiginous. I felt weak at the knees, and my brain was beginning to swim—a familiar feeling. The same sensation that I felt during our passionate encounter in my bedroom.

He looked down at me, eyes piercing mine.

I looked up at him submissively.

He then gave me the ultimatum. "I tell you what. You go home with me tonight, and I won't sleep with her—ever."

Suddenly, I heard someone clearing her voice. "Sorry, Trevor, I have to steal her away now. I have some friends upstairs who want to meet her. We'll see you later." Lori eyed Trevor with a keen coolness, took my arm, and we left.

As we took the stairs, Lori whispered, "Why didn't you tell me you two have the hots for each other?"

"It's not like that."

But Lori's expression was sarcastically saying—"yeah, right".

37

WALKING IN L.A.

"Ron! Hey! Forgive me, my name is Margee McGuire. I'm in a band called Scarlet White. I'm very sorry to bother you, but I have a demo here that I really think you'll like. If you could just give it a listen, I promise, you won't be disappointed. We're playing at The Roxy next weekend…"

Through his dark sunglasses, I could discern a vibe of annoyance, but he took the package and walked away without saying a word.

I spied him from a distance, and when Orion's senior A&R executive reached a trash receptacle, he brazenly dropped our promo package into it. My heart dropped as if it were being dumped in the trash as well.

For two hours prior, I had been on a stakeout. My eyes were on the entrance to Orion Records, awaiting my target, Ron Lubins. At 12:15 p.m., it took me by surprise to see him exit the building. Feeling like a stalker, I had followed him to a diner on Sunset, and waited until he finished his meal.

L.A. Word, a music and entertainment periodical, had recently published a special edition with a catalogue of A&R reps from Los Angeles, New York, and Nashville, featuring a bio and photo of the senior A&R executive, Ron Lubins of Orion Records. In my state of desperation, I made a poor decision to stalk Lubins and hand him our unsolicited demo. Humiliated, I drove back to Orange County with no clue of where to go from here. But by late October, Scarlet White would receive a ticket in.

Our new music, along with our image and stage presence, was effective. We tripled our following in just three months and began packing clubs consistently, and club managers were eager to book us back.

By the end of summer, a buzz was out on the streets about the new band, Scarlet White. Still, we were unable hook a single A&R executive. Although we did everything we thought was right, we continued to receive the same standard letter of rejection.

Early one August morning as I drove to work, I tuned in to an L.A. based radio station, KROC, when they announced that Geffen Records would be sponsoring a contest called Top of the ROC in search of the best L.A. band. The winner would receive a $75,000 recording contract, including management, tours, and a video. Five clubs in the L.A. and Orange County area would be participating in the competition by sending letters of referrals to Geffen Records of the three highest drawing bands between August and October, and those bands would have the opportunity to perform competitively on stage at the Vixen Theater in Hollywood in early December.

I was ecstatic, and at my first opportunity, I called Randy and asked him to contact KROC for details.

38

DON'T DREAM
IT'S OVER

"I love the scent of lilacs," I commented as we approached a flower stand. A few years back, I had tried to find a lilac perfume, but there was no perfume in existence that could successfully capture the heavenly, soft floral scent. Of course, the possibility that lilacs would be at the San Clemente Farmer's Market at the end of summer would be slight-to-nil, but I enjoyed inhaling fresh flowers, nevertheless.

As Brendan and I continued to browse, I had this feeling that something was on his mind; then he finally opened up. "Margee, I know you have your dream, but do you ever think about settling down?"

Brendan and I had kept our relationship discreet at work. But I was beginning to worry on several levels. I intuitively kept my relationship between the band and Brendan separate, unsure of how Randy would react. Then, there was the mental affair with Trevor. I was satisfied living in denial that Brendan was falling for me. However, now the cards were on the table. Unsure of how to respond, I said the first thing that rolled off my tongue. "Sure, one day."

"You know, Margee, I'm thirty-seven. I'm not like those young guys out there who are fine with having a fling. I want a meaningful relationship that has a chance to grow and flourish. and you and I... I think you love me, even though you won't admit it. I know you don't want to hear me say, 'I love you', so I won't say it. I can accept that. But the thing is, I just need to know. Where are we going with this?"

I allowed his message to steep. "Okay Brendan, I hear you. But I'm not ready for more. Will I ever be ready? I don't know."

I remained aloof the rest of the afternoon and made an excuse to go home early.

The following Monday at work, Brendan was apologetic. "Hey, Margee, I'm sorry about bringing up the commitment thing on Saturday. I know you're not ready, and now that I know where you stand, I'll respect that."

"It's okay, Brendan." I changed the subject. "Anyway, you want to go see a movie Friday night?"

"Actually, I have plans."

"Oh," I said, feeling abashed. Brendan had not made plans that didn't include me in the past six months. He had always kept his weekends open for me. If I were gigging on Friday and Saturday, we would meet for breakfast in the morning or spend the entire day together on Sunday. He responded delicately, as if trying to protect my feelings. "I used to be involved with this ski club, and I haven't really attended any of the meetings for several months, so I just thought I'd catch up with the group again. They're getting together to plan a trip in January."

My heart sank like a ship. But I maintained a cavalier exterior and offered a nonchalant response. "Okay. Well, have fun." I went to my car and sat for ten minutes to shed some tears before I came to my senses. This was my doing, and now I need to man up and accept the consequences of my actions.

39

EVERY BREATH YOU TAKE

"Hysteria" by Def Leppard resonated through the house speakers as we gathered around a long table. We were jovial, laughing, and cracking jokes with each other. It was Labor Day weekend, and we had just performed an afternoon gig at the Huntington Beach Pier Fest. The stage was grand, and bands of all different genres had performed throughout the day.

Street tacos and pitchers of margaritas were brought to the table to celebrate Greg's birthday. Trevor sat across from me on the opposite end of the table. And on two occasions, I glanced his way to meet his gaze. I finished my tacos and decided to cut the evening short.

Will had returned home for two months from his assignment in Japan. But early this morning, he left for Palm Springs to spend the weekend with some friends. During dinner, I had begun to worry about Duncan. Though I had given him enough food this morning to get him through the evening, I was worried about the ants.

Argentine ants, like humans, love the mild SoCal weather. They migrated here, theoretically, from New Orleans and began breeding at an insane rate. During the summer months, the ants enter the homes by the thousands scouting for food, and lately they had discovered Duncan's food bowl. Early this morning, I placed the cat food in a pedestal dessert bowl. I then placed the pedestal in another shallow bowl filled with water, creating a moat that the ants would have to swim through to get to the food.

Duncan was waiting for me on the back of the sofa. I kissed him twice on the top of his head, and then I went to check on his food. The moat had worked! There were a few scout ants around his bowl, but they couldn't make their way to his food.

As my eyes scanned the condo, I chuckled and shook my head. Will had tidied the condo a bit before he left. But I wasn't so sure it made much of a difference.

Will had several interests and projects that he tackled on an ongoing basis. He was an overachiever but didn't carry many of the classic type-A personality traits. He was easy going yet on a continuous journey to reach greater heights, insisting that most people waste their lives away when they could be doing so much more. "Margee, you just spent two hours cleaning the condo. You could have used that time practicing guitar."

"True," I had replied. "But you know, I can't focus on guitar when I'm sitting in a cluttered house."

Will's views on sleep were interesting. "Sleep is such a waste of time," he explained. "Think about all the hours people waste sleeping. When I go to bed, I listen to cassette tapes. That's how I'm learning to speak French. All I need is four hours of sleep."

"Dude, sleep is a time for rejuvenation," I countered. "Your body needs deep long sleep to recharge. Besides that," I pointed a finger and raised my eyebrows, "*you* need your beauty sleep." The bemused expression on his face tickled my heart as he pondered my statement and its intent.

Learning French was one of many of my brother's endeavors. He was also learning to play a Segovia piece on classical guitar, the art of the Japanese tea ceremony, as well as the martial art discipline of Shorin-Ryu. Most recently, he had taken a keen interest in the Dalai Lama, checking out stacks of books from the library in order to satisfy his obsession on the revered Tibetan monk. On top of all that, he had his projects from work. The books he brought home from the lab were thick, containing some sort of encrypted code and complex mathematical equations. And when anyone asked Will what he did at work, his playful response was always the same. "I can tell you, but within twenty-four hours you'll be classified as a missing person." To this day, I don't know what he does, because what he does really is highly classified, dealing with military weapons and warfare technology.

The only problem with Will's insatiable appetite for knowledge are the books, notebooks, cassettes, periodicals, and papers scattered all over the tables, counters, chairs, and even on the floor. Before he left for Palm Springs, he placed all his projects in neat stacks so one could argue that it looked better, but still, there were these stacks of literature, books, and notebooks on the counter, table, and sections of the floor.

I showered, combed my hair, and dried off when I heard the doorbell ring. I threw my bathrobe on to answer the door. It was Trevor. He was wearing my sunglasses. I had left them on the table at the restaurant. He pulled the sunglasses down his nose and was peering over them. "You forgot something."

I smiled. "Thank you, Trevor. I would hate to lose those."

He looked a little buzzed, and there was a bit of an awkward silence. "Mind if I use your bathroom?"

"Oh, sure. Come in."

I opened the door wide so he could enter. He crossed the threshold and stood behind me as I closed the door. When I turned, he took my arm gently and pulled me close. Without hesitation, I surrendered and wrapped my arms around him. We kissed. One kiss after another, each one better than the last, relentless, and this time I had no intention of stopping myself. I was beginning to transcend, until Trevor took a step back and lost his balance. He tripped over a stack of books on the floor and fell. On the way, he hit his head against the arm of a chair and let out a groan.

"Trevor! Are you okay? Oh my God, I'm so sorry! Will's stacks are all over the place!"

Trevor was on the floor holding his head. His eyes were scrunched closed. He opened his eyes slowly, and a single word came out of his mouth: "beauty".

I suddenly realized that my bathrobe had come undone, revealing my breast. I pulled the robe together.

"No. Don't do that," he whispered. Tenderly, he began pulling the robe apart.

He was tugging one way, and I was tugging the other.

"But you've seen *me* naked before," he whispered.

"That's different. You were hammered. And you're an exhibitionist." I stood up and offered my hand.

The next morning I awoke, transfixed on his face. He was so pretty. His lips were full, and his eyelashes were thick. His skin was healthy and smooth. He opened his eyes. They were sleepy, the lightest shade of brown, with the most unusual specks—topaz islands on amber planets. I could lose myself in them. He smiled.

40

HEROES

Fortuitously, our band had already booked three out of the five nightclubs participating in the Top of the ROC competition. Early September we played The Hot Spot in Huntington Beach, packing the house to a wildly enthusiastic audience. On September 12th, we performed at Madam Wong's West and sold out. And by mid-October, we performed at the Troubador in L.A., which to our surprise brought forth a positive review in *L.A. Word*.

Scarlet White Dazzles the Troubador

Scarlet White, fronted by female vocalist/guitarist, Margee McGuire, headlined Friday night to a sold-out crowd. McGuire opened the set striking devastating power chords followed by hypnotic vocals. Lead guitarist, Randy Carr, shreds. Other band members feature Trevor English on keyboards, Mike Hatfield on bass, and Greg Saffa on drums. The songs are well-written with great hooks, and the musicianship extraordinary. By the third song, the room was jumping. Keep your eyes open for this band and see them now, because they are going to bigger, better places.

We booked Bogart's in Long Beach on October 5th, which made four out of five clubs on the list. Even though we were unable to book The Roxy in time, we were confident that if we got four referrals, we would have our foot in the door.

On October 15th, the band gathered at Mike's apartment to hear KROC announce the finalists. Anxiety fused with excitement permeated the room like an odorless gas, while shots of Jose Cuervo neutralized the tension. One by one, the D.J., whose name was D.J. (Deacon Jones) revealed the contenders. "The day of reckoning is here! KROC, Killer Rock of Orange County, is just about to announce the winners of Top of the ROC! The first band to win the opportunity to perform at the Vixen on December 9th and a chance to compete for a $75,000 recording contract with Geffen Records is... Tesla!"

We were familiar with the first band but had never heard of the second band. After the second name was announced, we sat again in silence to hear the remaining bands. "The third band to compete at The Vixen in Hollywood is... Scarlet White!"

The band erupted in a euphoric frenzy, and my heart felt as though it was going to leap right out of my chest. My eyes welled. I was breathless. With all the excitement, we missed the name of the fourth band. But when the last band name was read, it struck me in the most peculiar and inexplicable way. "The last and final band to compete at The Vixen is... Tunnel Love!"

Did I really hear him say Tunnel Love? Maybe there was another band in L.A. or Orange County with that name. But two hours later, I received confirmation when my phone rang. It was Lori, and she was ecstatic. We congratulated each other, but my curiosity was digging at me. "Lori, to be honest, I was surprised to hear your band made it. You guys have only been together for four months. How did you do it?"

She explained that because her boyfriend, Dean, was sponsoring the band, they were able to rehearse four hours every day in a studio Dean leased in Hollywood. The money Dean had put into the band had allowed the members to quit their day jobs and focus primarily on tightening their music.

It would have taken quite a sum of money to support four musicians for several months. I couldn't imagine ever getting such a lucky break. To be able to quit my day job and just focus on music alone was a luxury I could only dream of. And then there was that night that Lori had intended to cheat on Dean with Trevor, and all the while Dean had been forking out so much money on her band. I wasn't sure whether Lori sensed a vibe of jealousy or slight resentment emanating over the wires, but her next words changed the course of my mental disparagement towards her. "Margee, you guys have come a long way. This is your time. Scarlet White is a tough act to beat, and everyone knows it. Anyway, it's a step closer for us."

"Thank you, Lori. I can't tell you how much that means to me, but you never know what the future holds. Anything is possible. Good luck. I wish you all the best."

The day after the radio announcement, we received a phone call from a Geffen representative, informing us that we would be receiving a package with instructions regarding the upcoming competition. Each band was to choose three songs to perform. To my dismay, I discovered that our band was first in the line-up. But we were not going to let that dampen our spirits or interfere with putting forth our best effort and greatest performance ever. We were confident and as ready as we would ever be.

Everything was going so well with the band. But there was now the extra complication with Trevor. He was on my mind constantly. I limited my outings with the band and avoided making too much eye contact with him at rehearsal. I was becoming more vulnerable, and he was aware of it.

One evening as I stood at the bar at Madame Wong's, Trevor approached me from behind and whispered in my ear. "Come home with me tonight, Margee, please." He gently brushed his lips along my ear, and his warm breath caused me to melt instantly.

I looked side-to-side to make sure the others were nowhere in sight and kept my back to him. "Remember, we talked about this Trevor. That night was a one-time thing. We can't make a habit of it."

"How about a two-time thing?"

41

HELLO, IT'S ME

As I approached my desk early Monday, I was surprised by a small cluster of lilac blooms with a note that read, "Congratulations Superstar!" It put a big smile on my face.

Although we continued to be amicable towards each other, Brendan and I had not been together since our commitment conversation at San Clemente.

I knocked gently on Brendan's office door before I entered with a bright smile. "Hi, so you heard?"

"Funny thing—I ran into Sanjoy yesterday at Golden Spoon and he filled me in. He's already making big plans to attend the Grammy awards with you next year. Got his outfit picked out and everything." We shared a good laugh, then Brendan added, "Congratulations. You deserve this."

"Thank you for the lilacs."

As I turned to leave, Brendan asked, "Can you get away for dinner tonight? We should celebrate."

I missed Brendan. I missed our deep conversations and his way of making me laugh. I missed our foodie restaurant dates. With little hesitation, I accepted. "Sure. That sounds nice."

In a snap, Brendan and I reunited. "Look Margee," he conveyed, "whether there's a future with you or not, I still want to spend as much time with you as I can if that's okay. I enjoy your companionship."

We both knew there would come a day when we would have to go our separate ways, and little tinges of guilt would shake its finger at my better half for reigniting the relationship. But if there was something real between us, it would survive the test of separation and time. Any reason to believe that I might be using Brendan to keep myself away from Trevor was tossed in the river of denial.

In November, I invited Brendan over for Thanksgiving where he met my mother, my brothers Daniel, Will, and Cory along with Daniel's wife, Jules, Will's fiancé, Izumi, and Cory's California girlfriend number six, Kelly. Naturally, everyone fell in love with Brendan, including, my oldest brother, Daniel.

Daniel wasn't necessarily a people person. He was unforgiving of any character traits that would indicate fraud. It was as though he had some built-in sensor that went off when a pretentious person entered his space, as he could only tolerate authentic souls. But the most intriguing thing about Daniel is that he is a genius in the literal sense of the word. At eighteen, he picked up an electric guitar and started playing a Jimi Hendrix solo, note for note. This was during the days when Hendrix was at the top of his game. And at the time, only Jimi could play like Jimi. Daniel graduated from college early with a doctorate degree in physics. But typical of those with the gift of genius, Daniel had difficulty managing the simple things in life like getting to work on time or returning a phone call. I had always thought that if Daniel had someone to manage his day-to-day affairs, he would have accomplished astounding feats in science or invention. But most employers didn't understand in the early '70s that Daniel's brain was wired only for complexity. Daniel didn't have a lackadaisical attitude towards getting ahead in life like some had erroneously thought. The truth was Daniel had the mental capacity to do what the average person couldn't fathom, so simple daily duties were too trivial to matter. Eventually, Daniel landed a job at a research lab for an insightful employer who recognized Daniel's gift and accepted his shortcomings. Because I respected and looked up to Daniel to such a high degree, his opinion meant a great deal. Like the others, Daniel accepted Brendan.

Brendan listened with his heart and his head, soaking in every word like a song. This quality gave him the ability not only to read people, but also to know how to choose the right response to win people over. His feedback often offered comfort, clarity, and assurance for whatever the case may be. Because Brendan was so well grounded and secure with himself, others gravitated to him. These qualities, coupled with Daniel's stamp of approval, fostered Brendan's pull on me.

I was beginning to spend much more time with Brendan. In fact, so much more, that friends and family considered us a pair. Although I had kept my relationship with Brendan separate from the band, he expressed a strong desire to see and support our band the night of the competition, especially an event that could very well be a turning point for my future.

42

HERE'S WHERE THE STORY ENDS

I hardly slept on the eve of the competition. This was it. After today, Scarlet White would be signed. I was sure of it, as long as we were flawless like our last three rehearsals. Not only would be have to be flawless, we would also need to deliver the performance of our lives.

Brendan and I decided to stay overnight in Hollywood. We checked in to our hotel at The Roosevelt and arrived at sound check at 2:45 p.m.

Performing at The Vixen was a milestone for any up-and-coming act. Typically, only signed bands, accomplished comedians, and first-class theatrical productions performed in this small-scale theatre, and the patrons had to pay quite a bit to have the luxury of viewing the celebrities up close in such an intimate setting.

The ground level was speckled with mounted fan-shaped cocktail tables for parties of two or three with a great view of the stage. The upper balcony located in the rear consisted of stadium seating. And beneath the upper balcony, ground level, was a long bar made of burlwood serving the finest spirits and hand-crafted signature cocktails. Two levels of scalloped booths for private parties up to six were located on both east and west wings. Built in the late 1920s, The Vixen had great bones. The decor was an eclectic mix of antique and modern. Twelve enormous waterfall crystal chandeliers graced the theater. Decorated in rich peacock blue, midnight blue, and gold, The Vixen was an interior designer's delight and a treat for the eyes at every angle.

When the rest of the band arrived, I introduced them to Brendan, and my foreboding concern about revealing my boyfriend to the band was legitimized when the axe came down on Randy's heart. So obvious was his jealousy, that the atmosphere turned frigid and regret rained down on me. Presenting Brendan to the band on this day was a stupid mistake. Mike offered to talk to Randy with my support. "Mike, you have to help Randy see the big picture. If we win, Randy can have Heather Locklear for God's sake. If he blows this, he will be kicking himself in the ass for the next twenty years."

The rest of the band was very polite towards Brendan—all except Trevor. Trevor shook Brendan's hand curtly. He didn't smile or make much eye contact. He separated from the band until sound check. I was well aware of his distance.

The situation was delicate. The thought of Trevor being with Lori made me miserable. I wondered if I was subjecting Trevor to the same suffering. I had always assumed that Trevor was a player—a young guy out to get a little action from an older girl. He couldn't possibly have any real feelings for me other than young lust. Or could he? What if I meant more to Trevor than I realized? I felt an injection of guilt, the worst emotion in my book of emotions, and I scolded myself: *Not today, Margee. Today is not the day to torment yourself with your mental battles.*

"Good job," the sound technician complimented after we checked our levels and played our opening song. "You guys are going to kill it tonight."

A great sound check is always a confidence booster for a band. The offerings of approval from the staff and other bands lingering in the auditorium are always a good sign. They hear bands all the time. If they're impressed, it validates that everything is going to be all right. Both the PA system and the technician were phenomenal. I couldn't remember ever sounding so good.

Afterward, Brendan and I went back to our hotel. On a normal day, I can devour my lion's share of food, but hours prior to a performance, my appetite vanishes. Brendan had not eaten since early morning, and he insisted that I remain in the room to run over the set and relax while he went out to order a burger at the Sunset Grill.

In the meantime, I prepared for the show. This was a sacred time for me. I soaked in a steamy bath, and it calmed me to the bone. The process of applying my makeup was meditative as I transitioned into the artist mode, focusing on my face, the canvas. I placed the same amount of meticulous care towards styling my hair.

When we arrived at The Vixen, I was pumped up and greeted the band. Lights flashed as we posed for photographs. Although nervous, we were in high spirits. Brendan took a seat with a group of co-workers from Urban Perspective. We were instructed to go backstage where a tall Jamaican with dreadlocks led us to our dressing room. We ruminated about how anxious we felt. This is about the time that my nerves start to wreak havoc on my digestive system, sending my metabolism into overdrive. It never fails. I had to take several trips to the bathroom to eliminate the product of my anxiety. How thankful I was that the moment we were on, my anxieties would vanish. It was the anticipation. The anticipation was always the worst.

Ten minutes later, the tall Jamaican poked his head through our dressing room door. "Everything okay back here?" He raised his hand with fingers spread. "Five minutes."

Trevor handed us each a second shot of tequila. I raised my glass. "I just want to say I really love you guys. You're my family. We deserve this. And we're going to win. Let's go out there and kick ass!"

"Here, here," they toasted.

We received another knock on the door. The Jamaican peered through once again and solemnly made his announcement. "It's time."

We approached the stage single file.

In a few seconds, the shimmer-sheer navy curtain panel in front of us would rise, and we would be on. In front of the panel, an emcee from KROC was rousing the audience, though I had difficulty making out some of the words, until he raised his voice in the end and finished with our cue. "Please welcome, Scarlet White!"

Trevor began with a sequence emulating the sound of a helicopter far in the distance gradually getting closer and louder as the panel lifted. The audience erupted. Followed by Trevor's sequence, in gradual layers, were bass and drums, then guitars. Up to this point, the sound was dead on, but when I began singing, there was a problem—*a major problem.*

The vocals were non-existent through my monitor and barely audible through the mains. After the first verse, I could see the confusion in their faces. The audience could not hear my vocals. It was extremely distracting. The beginning of the end. The audio engineer was frantically checking the board to locate the problem. Then came the feedback, and still through the entire song, barely any vocals. We began our second song. The engineer was now on stage checking the mains and monitors! By the end of the second song, the vocals were finally coming through the mains, but I couldn't hear my vocals at all through the monitors, so I wasn't sure if I was singing on key. Greg, who depended on vocal cues on certain parts, had to play by sheer memory and guitar cues, counting measures to decipher where we were in the song, sacrificing feel. At one point, I lost focus, fumbled, and played a bad chord on the second song. The feedback continued to pierce through, on and off, through the third song. The activity onstage by the audio engineer was a huge distraction and a detriment to our show. The chaos interfered with my stage presence, and my disappointment had begun to swallow me whole. When we ended our third and final song, the five of us stood together center stage and bowed to a more-than-gracious audience. This performance, which was supposed to be our finest, turned out to be the worst performance I could ever recall, not only with this band, but the worst performance of my entire life, and I was devastated. How could this have possibly happened when the sound check just a few hours earlier was so close to perfection?

There was a fifteen-minute intermission before the next band. I rushed over to speak to the sound engineer. "What the hell? What happened?"

"To be quite honest, I don't know. Fifteen years in this business. This is the first time something like this has ever happened. Someone switched the cables around on the board. Fuck!"

"What about the monitors? I couldn't hear my vocals through them!"

"The cables were pulled out of the monitors."

It took me a moment to comprehend what the sound engineer had just told me. He was frantically preparing for the next act. "Look, Margee, I don't know what to say. I'm sorry, but I'm really busy right now. I've got to get this shit straightened out."

I returned to our dressing room with a heavy heart, struggling to hold in the tears. I remained there through the next two bands when Trevor peered through the door. "Hey there. I've been looking for you."

I didn't want to talk about it. With elbows on the dressing table, my hands were clasped together, holding my head. He sat on my bench, and I felt his hand caress my shoulder. Muted music hovered in the background when Trevor saw a tear drop to the vanity.

"Come here, Margee," he whispered.

I threw my arms around him and nestled into him. He rubbed my back and nuzzled my hair. At that very moment, I could feel only him and nothing else, and I wanted to hold on to that moment forever. I wanted to fall asleep and never wake up, cradled by him—protected, as if in mother's arms for all eternity.

"Margee, don't give up. You can't assume we didn't win."

Suddenly Randy entered the room and shook me from my reverie. "Is everything okay?"

"It's okay," Trevor replied.

"Lori is going on right now. I thought Margee wanted to see her."

"We'll be out in a minute, Randy," Trevor replied.

Randy left.

I composed myself. "Thank you, Trevor. Let's go see Lori."

Trevor and I walked to the side stage, and this was the moment when I felt as though I'd entered the twilight zone. Aside from Lori's platinum blond hair and her all-black color scheme, she wore a similar ensemble to mine: knee-high Doc Martens and a short silk slip dress. But her guitar was a custom bubble-gum pink Strat, which Dean must have bought for her. Her hair was tousled like the main of a wild horse. And her eyeliner was heavy and black, extra-thick underneath the eyes. It gave her a progressive, Gothic edge. The contrast between the black of her eyes and her platinum hair was dramatic. When it was time for Tunnel Love to perform, all the kinks had been worked out of the PA system, and it seemed to be fully recovered from its mysterious debacle. The audience roared for her, and her spirits were as high as the heavens, giving her the confidence of a well-seasoned diva. Although her guitar was just a façade for the most part, the audience never knew it. Her guitar volume had been purposely turned down, so when she struck a chord it was barely audible. All her guitar parts were doubled by another guitarist in her band. But the beast that branded my soul were the songs she played. The three songs Lori had chosen to play were my songs: the same old songs from my red notebook that we played in her apartment at Newport Beach not so long ago.

A sick feeling enveloped me. Still, foolishly I thought, maybe we have a chance. Surely the judges would realize that Scarlet White was the better band that had just suffered from some technical issues that we had no control over.

When Lori's band finished, she had an entourage surrounding her backstage, including Sanjoy. Dean hugged her and presented her with a bouquet of pink roses.

There was a twenty-minute intermission for deliberation, and the winner was announced. Tunnel Love would be signed by Geffen Records. Lori had achieved in six months what I couldn't in fifteen years.

I took Brendan's hand. "Let's go." The barrage of emotions was too overwhelming to suppress: humiliation, shame, anger, despair. I felt cheated and betrayed. On the drive to the hotel, I didn't say a word. Instead, I cried like a boy, silently. I held the tears in as best as I could. But every now and then, one forced its way down my cheek, and I discreetly brushed it away.

Brendan dropped me off at the hotel. But before he returned to The Vixen to retrieve my gear, he hugged me tightly. He didn't know what to say, but it seemed as though he was suffering too, as though he understood the pain that I felt. "I'd give anything to make you feel better, Margee."

I believed him, but there was nothing to give.

On the ride back to Orange County, Brendan told me that the best thing for me right now was to get away from it all. "Let's take a trip—somewhere nice and tropical. We can lie on the beach in the Caribbean, stay at some five-star resort, get a massage under a palm tree...drink out of coconut shells. We should go right away. In fact, I'll take some time off for Christmas."

At that moment, I was ready to run away, so I managed a weak smile. But there was business to take care of first.

43

YOU OUGHTA KNOW

I tracked down Rob, the sound engineer at The Vixen, to discuss the events that took place between our sound check and our performance. Apparently, the sound check for each band was fine, but somehow, between the sound check and the first band, someone had tampered with the sound system. The cables to the PA system that were supposed to be plugged into the main inputs had been switched to the monitor inputs. This was done for both right and left mains. In addition to that, the cables had been pulled out of the socket, loose on the left main speaker, so that it appeared to be pushed in at first glance. That's why it took so long to figure out why they were not producing any sound. This had also been done with two of the monitors. The only source of sound would have been coming through the left monitor and the right main. Rob mentioned that some of the knobs and sliders on the board had been altered as well. He was profusely apologetic. "Someone must have come into the club after the all the sound checks were done. I don't know why. I don't know who would do something this shitty."

"Do you remember who was hanging around the theater after the last sound check?"

Rob rubbed his fingers tentatively across his goatee. "When I left, there were four, no, five people still there: a photographer and the journalist from *L.A. Word,* but they were packing up, and I saw them leave when I got in my car. The only other people left inside were Lourdes Love and her friend—some Indian guy. Peter was there too...in the office. I don't remember anyone else."

The Indian must have been Sanjoy. Peter, the club owner, had no motive to sabotage the PA system. He would have wanted a great sound for all the bands that night. Sanjoy was out of the question. But, Lori….she was the smoking gun. She was the only one who had a motive. My band was first to perform, and her band was last. This would have given the sound engineer plenty of time to work out all the kinks. She had taken everything else from me—my image *and* my songs. She could have easily done it in less than five minutes while Sanjoy was in the restroom or even after he left. All this time, her dumb blonde exterior had been an act to cover her conniving ulterior motives.

I began to recall my experiences with her. Cory had always believed that she stole Devon's necklace. She ran from restaurants without paying. She had every intention to cheat on Dean after he had financed her entire band for months. It began to dawn on me. When she wants something, she takes it. It doesn't matter who she hurts or ruins along the way. She knew Scarlet White was favored to win. To sabotage our performance would have given her the upper hand. She saw a crack in the door that would catapult her life to a level that would be unimaginable otherwise. A rock star lifestyle would have suited her racy disposition, and when desperation sinks its teeth into our souls, it bites down and breaks the best of us. I can only imagine that the worst of us would heed no hesitation or suffer any compromise of conscience. She would have kicked open the door and seized her prize. The more I thought about it, the more it made sense, and my blood began to boil.

44

PSYCHO KILLER

It was early Sunday, and I knew she'd still be in bed. I wanted to catch her before she left, because I needed to have a "few" words with her. After five minutes of pounding, Dean opened the door with an expression of hostility, followed by surprise. "Margee."

I managed a fake smile. "Is Lori home?"

"Yeah, uh… Just a minute," Dean replied with uncertainty.

I discerned movement in the hall when Lori came into view and stood beside Dean with sleepy, puppy dog eyes, and her tone was that of compassion and surprise. "Margee—"

"How could you do it, Lori?"

Lori had always been a good actress. I had witnessed her fake tears and seen her feign illness and turn on the charm to get what she wanted. Confused, she scrunched her face. "What?"

"You *know* what, Lori, and I'm not buying your bullshit, so cut the act. You fucked up the sound system at the Vixen and sabotaged our performance. You pulled cables. And on top of that you stole my songs. How could you stoop so low?"

Like a flick of a switch, her angelic demeanor vanished, and she fired back indignantly. "I don't know what the fuck you're talking about. You were never going to use those songs anyway. You said they lacked—oh what was your word—*integrity*. Yeah, that's it, because you're so God damned perfect and above it all. You could have never imagined in a thousand years that I could ever outdo you. I knew what you were thinking all along: 'Lori's a loser. She'll never be able stand up to me.' But I did, and you're not going to fucking rain on my parade."

"Lori, don't you get it? Those were *my* songs you played. You beat me using *my* songs."

"You threw those songs away. You were never going to use them! Anyway, I changed those songs up."

"Adding an instrumental break or changing a couple words is not changing it up. You're either too stupid to realize it, or you don't have an ounce of—yeah, that word—integrity or honor to fess up to it. What you did to me was the height of betrayal. The bottom line is you stole my songs *and* my lifelong dream!"

"Oh yeah, prove it! Because guess what? I have the copyrights to those songs now, bitch!"

She was yelling. I was seething. How could she speak to me that way? She was the one who stabbed *me* in the back. We entered into a heated fury, hollering at the top of our lungs.

"Do you realize what you did," I hissed. "I spent fifteen years of my life working towards this goal, and you spent six months!"

"I worked hard these last six months! You have no idea!"

"You have no concept of hard work! You never did! The only thing you've worked hard at these past six months was spreading your legs!"

Lori's eyes widened, so much that the whites showed around the circumference of her iris. She rushed through the door and shoved me with both hands out to the lawn. I stumbled back but quickly found my ground. I hauled off and slapped her hard across her face. She threw a punch at mine, but I ducked and threw my shoulders into her chest, which brought us both down to the ground. We landed on a slope and rolled down to the bottom of the yard until Lori ended up on top of me. I gripped her shirt with both hands and head-butted her on the bridge of her nose. Warm drops of blood dripped on my face. She punched my left eye.

Throughout our brawl, Dean was shouting. "Stop! Stop it! Lourdes! Margee!"

Suddenly, Dean and a neighbor managed to separate us. Lori and I were slumped over in exhaustion, panting, heaving. I screamed at her bloody face with blood and tears running down mine. "I never want to see you again! Ever!" I broke free from my restrainer's grip and stormed away.

In the distance, I could hear Lori screaming. "You never believed in me! I could see it in your eyes and hear it in your voice! Well, fuck you!"

I woke up Monday morning with my left eye swollen black and blue, the same as my wounded spirit. I had hardly slept, so I called in sick at work. To make matters worse, Scarlet White received a bashing in *L.A. Word* for our performance at The Vixen. Most of the criticism pointing towards lead singer, Margee McGuire, whose voice couldn't carry.

Our band decided to take two months off in December, and Brendan proceeded to make arrangements for our trip to the Caribbean.

But the echoes of my fight with Lori continued to plague me. And fate would contradict my words, "I never want to see you again!" Because I *would* see Lori again and again, whether I liked it or not, at the grocery stand and on television. And I would hear her voice across the radio waves singing my songs. Songs that were now hers, or at least that's what the rest of the world would believe.

PART TWO

45

FOLLOW YOUR BLISS

On a rainy weekend in early January, I had just finished running some errands when I arrived home to find my mother, along with her friend, Chiko, at the condo chatting with Will. Will had returned from his six-month assignment in Italy and had moved back home temporarily to prepare for his next assignment in Hawaii. As I entered the condo, I could hear them conversing in Japanese. We greeted, and they began speaking in English. I had never learned to speak Japanese, because my father believed that learning two languages would hinder my ability to learn English properly. This rationale seemed to be more the norm in those days. Will, however, had learned to speak Japanese on his own accord in high school, and he became fluent.

My mother was never able pronounce my name correctly. It came out sounding more like Moggy. She spoke with enthusiasm about my new boyfriend, Brendan, which came out sounding more like Bulenda. "Moggy have very nice, rich, handsome boyfriend. He take her to nice vacation to beautiful beach some far away country!"

Chiko raised her eyebrows and pressed the corners of her lips down as if very impressed. "Why he not ask you to marry, Moggie?"

"He's waiting for me to give him the green light."

With that, my mother interjected. "Why you not give green light? Red light no good for girl your age. You thirty years old. He handsome. He good looking. He rich. He such a nice, sweet guy!" For years, my mother had always supported my musical endeavors. It was my luck she had never seen me perform, except for Scarlet White's concert at the Vixen. Years and years of impressive near-perfect performances with a great mix, but my mother was to see the worst performance of my life. So now she had changed her tune. "You know, Moggy, more to life than just music. What about nice husband and family? You be very happy with baby. I'm so happy when you born. Even though Daddy leave me, I still so happy to have all my babies. I never regret. Now you and your brothers grown up, and I still so happy and proud."

I opened the fridge to get my second beer.

The conversation switched back to Japanese. Mom made flamboyant hand gestures as she sashayed around the living room, entertaining Chiko and Will as they chuckled at her theatrics. I heard my mother mention Sanjoy's name. Later, I asked Will what she said.

"Mom cracks me up. She thinks Sanjoy was your boyfriend before Brendan."

46

HUMAN ON THE INSIDE

"Because we sucked at the Vixen! And now we have a bad reputation! And it's not you and me, is it?" Randy shouted. "It's you and Mr. executive...or Trevor! Tell me, Margee! Which one is it?"

When Brendan and I returned from the Caribbean, I felt rejuvenated and ready to pick up the pieces to put Scarlet White back together again. Our tropical escape was the first time I had ever traveled anywhere outside the country, and the experience was monumental. But the perfect peaks of my Caribbean bliss were overshadowed by the dark valley of loss, shame, and heartbreak that was just around the bend. Like a standing line of dominos, all it took was for one to fall.

On our first rehearsal after the Vixen fiasco, Randy brought along his new girlfriend, Dayna. They arrived arm in arm, giggling. Randy was giddy and behaving strangely. In the past, he would agree with nearly all my suggestions, but on this night, he was disagreeable and challenged me on every point and issue.

I also got a bad vibe from Dayna, a petite blonde with seven-inch heels, a tight miniskirt, and a puffy white bolero jacket. Her blue eyes, surrounded by a thick coat of black mascara and eyeliner, pierced me like icicles, as she scrutinized me through two evil almond slits.

In the past two years, as the band became more serious, we realized that we needed an environment conducive to strengthening our music, where band members had the freedom to be creative and interact with each other with no outside interference. So closed rehearsals (band members only) became the norm.

When rehearsal ended, I wanted to pull Randy aside to speak to him. But I couldn't find the opportunity. I took a quick trip to the bathroom, but when I returned, Randy had already packed up his guitar. When I reached the parking lot, I could see him in the distance sucking face with Dayna in a ridiculous public display.

Later that night, I phoned Randy to speak to him about our closed rehearsal policy. "Randy, what's up with bringing a date to rehearsal?"

"She's not a date. She's my girlfriend. We're serious."

"Okay, that's fine. But rehearsals should be closed, shouldn't they?"

"Margee, you're talking like you're jealous."

"Randy, if you were my brother, I'd still be having this conversation. This has nothing to do with jealousy. It's business. During rehearsal we work, we create…with no outside distractions. If you worked in an office, you wouldn't bring your girlfriend with you to your desk to watch you work, right? After rehearsal, fine, you can do whatever you want with your significant other. But there's a time and place for these things."

"First of all, Dayna isn't just some random girl I brought in to show off. She works in the music business. She manages bands and has seen all the bands in Orange County and L.A. She knows what's cool and what's not. She knows the ins-and-outs of the business. She can help us. And the only way she can do that is to be involved with the band."

"Oh, is that right? So...she's, like a band member now. You just figured you could take it upon yourself without anyone's consent to bring in a new member."

"Every now and then someone else in the band can make an executive decision besides you, Margee."

"What are you talking about? I don't make executive decisions for this band."

"Oh yeah? Well, what about the band image, the band name, the musical arrangements?"

"What the hell are you talking about? I made suggestions, and I thought we all agreed. I'm trying to get us a record deal."

"Okay, and now Dayna can help us, because your way didn't work."

"So that's how it's going to be? What's her opinion about me? I can't wait to hear this."

It didn't take a genius to figure out that Dayna despised every molecule of my being for whatever reason. Randy hesitated for several seconds to gather his courage. "Dayna was at the Vixen that night."

"What the fuck is that supposed to mean?"

"Never mind, Margee."

"No!" I blurted. Then somehow, I regained an ounce of composure. "Don't tell me never mind. Tell me what you mean." I felt my anxiety swell as my heart rate began to rise, and this would have been a good time to end the conversation. But I was young with far too much passion to have the maturity to blow it off and move on. Had Greg been involved in the conversation, he would have intervened, smoothed everything out.

But Randy's foolishness had pushed me beyond my limit, and my hostility had pierced Randy, so he unloaded. "The reviews at the Vixen were not good. They called us the *Titanic*. We seemed phenomenal to begin with, but now we're a sinking ship. And I don't know how committed I want to be to a sinking ship. I've been in this band for a long time, and maybe it's time for me to move on."

"I suppose Dayna has nothing to do with your complete 180-degree change of heart towards this band."

"To be honest with you, Dayna thinks that the rest of the band is not up to my level. She thinks I should audition for other bands—optimize my options. She's already lined me up with another band that has an amazing lead singer who sounds just like Steve Perry."

I could feel the walls closing in on me. My closest ally was turning against me. I tried to compose myself, chill my temper. I had to convince him—bring him back to me. "Randy, just one month ago we were the hottest band in Southern California. Some setbacks are to be expected in life. That doesn't mean you give up. Besides, you know that night had nothing to do with our talent or skill. There were technical issues with the sound system. It wasn't our fault, Randy."

"It definitely wasn't my fault!"

"Are you saying that what happened at the Vixen was my fault?"

"Look, Margee, Dayna knows a lot of people. And she knows what she's talking about. I've spent a long time in this band and gotten nowhere."

"Randy, listen to yourself. You aren't the only one who's invested time. We *all* invested time *and* money. Besides, if you've invested so much time into this band, how can you think about leaving now, when we were so close? We can make it happen. I know it. We started Scarlet White together, you and me—our songs. What is it that you want from me? I'll do anything to keep this band together! Dude, we're the heart and soul of this band. How can you think about throwing it all away after all we've been through?"

"Because we sucked at the Vixen! And now we have a bad reputation! And it's not you and me, is it? It's you and Mr. executive…or Trevor! Which one is it, Margee? And all this time you said that you would never have a relationship within the band because it would sacrifice our success. Well, guess what, Margee? It's not you and me anymore. Now, it's Dayna and me. And *you* sacrificed the success of the band, Margee! *You!*"

I couldn't for the life of me hold my tongue, and I exploded internally. But somehow kept a cool exterior. On the verge of bursting into tears, I managed a vulgar closure. "You know, Randy, you're a pussy-whipped, brainwashed idiot." In my fury, I slammed the phone down. I picked it up and slammed it down again and again and broke my phone. I was unaware that I was crying until I noticed droplets of tears rain down to the carpet. I tried to divert my mind towards something else, anything else. Was I going crazy? The truckloads of disappointment dumped on me, one after the other, had pushed me over the edge. I had never lost my cool so severely before, and I felt deeply ashamed.

The following day Randy phoned Mike and told him that he was leaving the band. Curious, the other guys asked me what happened. I didn't want to talk about it, but I owed them an explanation, so I selectively recapped our conversation. Mike felt as though I had reacted harshly. He suggested that I apologize to Randy, but my pride would not allow it. In just two and a half months, two bridges had been burned. Two people I loved, who I thought would always love me, were no longer a part of my life.

47

ORDINARY WORLD

I t was a somber winter. Greg, Mike, and Trevor didn't adopt the same negative attitude as Randy. In fact, they stood behind me, and the Scarlet White project, one-hundred percent. They wanted to put the past behind and move forward, and begin auditioning lead guitarists at once.

Greg had the task of pumping up my broken ego. I was beginning to doubt myself and questioned whether I was cut out for this. I started to dwell on my poor reviews and my last conversation with Randy. Not only that, I had come to a fork in the road of my life. I stood there for a long time, looking one way and then the other. I began to rethink my future—what it would look like? And it was the first time I have ever contemplated it so negatively. I cringed at the thought of being thirty-five and still playing grungy dives with the off-color smell of old cigarette smoke and grimy stained carpet. In the light of day, the reality of these small-time venues showed its face like an aged drag queen with harsh makeup. I had always thought that by thirty I would at least be playing upscale clubs and theatres like The Vixen or

The Joint in Vegas. But things happen for a reason. What was the reason for our failure at the Vixen? Was it providence trying to tell me something? Greg, Mike, and Trevor were several years younger than me. They still had a huge window of opportunity, but my window was starting to close. We would have to start all over again. It would take another six months to a year to find someone to fill Randy's shoes and to tighten up the band enough to perform up to the same standard as before. I couldn't go backwards. I was beside myself, and I felt alone in my conflict.

On the other hand, I had invested years of my life towards this goal, and it was the only life I had ever really known. So I couldn't give up, and Scarlet White proceeded to audition guitarists—but it didn't go well. I kept comparing everyone to Randy, and there would never be another Randy. He was exceptional—leagues above all the rest. And he had been able to sing backups in perfect pitch even while playing a hook or a fill. By the end of spring, we were still unable to find a suitable guitarist to replace Randy. I felt as though Scarlet White was hanging by a thread.

In early August, the thread weakened. Mike announced that he would be relocating to Northern California. He had fallen in love with a girl in the Bay area that he met at a wedding reception three months earlier, and he had been offered a job with her company. It was a difficult decision for him, but it just so happened that the girl he had fallen for was a drummer, so he followed the beat of his heart. Now, we were down to three.

The band and several friends decided to have a going away party for Mike. We gathered at the Rooftop Bar and Grill in Laguna Beach for drinks. Located at the top of the Laguna Azul Hotel, we reminisced about good times and sipped cocktails against the setting sun. I made the mistake of drinking one too many designer martinis. Around 10:30 p.m., I stumbled out of the bar. Concerned, Greg asked Trevor to drive me home.

Trevor caught up to me. "Hey... Margee, let me drive you home."

"Oh yeah, and you're better off?"

"Much better off."

I held up my pointer finger and declared, "*I'm* the responsible one. *I* book the gigs, *I* do all the promotion, *I* create the fliers, *I* send out the fliers, *I* maintain the mailing list. *I* do all the research on record labels. *I* send out the demos—"

"I don't know what we'd do without you, Margee."

He put his arm around my shoulder as we walked to the parking lot, and I placed both arms around him. I was slurring and talking drunken nonsense. "Did you know you are the prettiest boy I have ever slept with? Your lips are pretty. Your eyes are pretty. I bet a lot of gay guys are attracted to you."

"Thanks?" he responded with uncertainty.

"Hey, let's go someplace," I said. "I know a dance club just down the road."

"No way, young lady. I think you've had quite enough for one night. I'm going to take you home and tuck you in."

"Good, and I'm going to love on you tonight."

Trevor chuckled. "I love it when you're drunk, Margee."

"I'm going to love *and* ravish you."

"Margee! You make me feel so cheap, like a piece of meat. Can't we just hold each other tonight?"

I laughed at Trevor's jest. When we reached the car, I pushed him against the door and pressed up against him. We kissed.

Trevor brushed my hair out of my face with his fingers.

"Seriously, Margee, I don't want to take advantage. You've had a lot to drink. But I will stay with you if you want me to."

I stepped back from Trevor, hands on my hips. "*Yes*, I want you to." I held my pointer finger up and attempted to sway it back and forth in the soul sister fashion, but I didn't quite carry the sister swagger. Instead, I carried a drunken stagger. "Let's just get this straight. You're not the one taking advantage. I am. I'm taking advantage of you—older woman taking advantage of a younger man."

With his right fist over his mouth, and right elbow resting on the other fist, Trevor's eyebrows were arched. "Whatever you say, boss. I won't argue with that. You do whatever you want to me."

I wrapped my arms around him and squeezed him tight.

He reciprocated. "But what about your boyfriend, Mr. executive?"

Oh, my God, I thought. Randy called him that too. The thought of Brendan made me sober up a bit. "We're not married, Trevor."

We got into Trevor's car and continued the conversation as I defended myself. "Why is it that a guy can go sex around with two or more girls, and it's okay, but when a girl does it, there's something wrong with it?"

"Well, I think it doesn't matter who is doing it—girl or guy— if there are going to be hearts broken, or if one of the parties believes there is a commitment or a serious thing going on. *Maybe* it's wrong? I'm just saying *maybe*."

"Trevor, I had no idea you were so gallant. So, are you telling me that you don't want to have sex with me because it could be wrong?"

"No, no, no, no. I never said that. Now don't go putting words in my mouth. Maybe we should change the subject. It's none of my business anyway, your situation. I was a complete idiot for bringing it up." Sensibly, Trevor changed the subject. "Now let me see you put your hands on your hips like you did before, sway your shoulders back and forth, and tell it like it is, girl."

I sat erect, pointer finger up, and gave him a little show. We both cracked up.

We decided it best to go to Trevor's place instead of mine since he lived just a half mile up the road. But when we got there, I felt queasy. I ran to the bathroom to unload my last two drinks.

"How many martinis did you drink?" Trevor asked.

"Four."

"What! Are you kidding me. What did you eat today?"

"I had a bowl of Raisin Bran for breakfast."

"That's it? No wonder you got so shit-faced."

Trevor made me a grilled cheese sandwich that I devoured along with a ginger ale. It was the best grilled cheese sandwich I had ever eaten in my entire life.

"Now go brush your teeth before I give you a smack bottom." Trevor twirled a kitchen towel between two hands and snapped one end towards my butt. I squeaked and scurried to the bathroom.

As I brushed my teeth, I could hear Trevor cleaning the kitchen. On a whim, I decided to take a bath in his claw-footed vintage bathtub.

When Trevor entered the bathroom, he found me soaking in the tub. "My, I dare say, what a beautiful mermaid! May I join you?

"Yes, you may, beautiful merman!"

"I'm very shy, so you must close your eyes."

I put my hands over my eyes, but spread my fingers wide and peeked through. "I'm not peeking," I said in my Austin Powers accent, then giggled at myself.

His body was beautiful. He was tall and tan from the surf. His biceps were defined, but not bulky. His tummy was lean and sculpted. He stepped into the tub and sat down. The water flowed over the edge. "Oh, shit!"

We giggled as I reached over the tub to grab a towel and throw it down to the floor to soak up the water. When I went to sit back down, he had taken my spot, so I sat on top of him, my back to his chest, like nestling spoons. He gave me little kisses and nibbles on my ear.

The following morning Trevor drove me to my car. He was sweet and playful, but I was feeling guilty, which I passed off as being hung over. We talked about the band, and I told him about my feelings, the long journey, and starting over again. But Trevor had taken a more positive attitude than me. "We did it before.

We'll do it again. I'm sure of it. But I can't say how long it will take. Besides, I never really liked Randy's style of guitar playing anyway. I don't think we need a guitarist who can shred like Yngwie Malmsteen. Hooks are the future. You know—updating the Jimmy Page thing. People don't want to hear speed lead anymore."

48

STRAWBERRY ROAD

I was weaving an intricate web and getting tangled up in it. I had officially cheated on Brendan, and I had always considered this type of behavior deplorable. I had broken the divide between professionalism in the band and entered into an intimate relationship with Trevor. So now, I had to decide, once and for all, to make a choice to either break up with Brendan or never sleep with Trevor again. But when my decision was made, it didn't matter, because the last thread holding Scarlet White together broke in early September when I discovered I was pregnant.

For the first time in my life, I could no longer put myself first.

When I told Brendan about the pregnancy, his immediate response was joy. Then his demeanor shifted to desperation. "What will you do?"

"I'm up for suggestions."

Brendan appeared to be on the brink of tears. "Margee, what this baby needs is a mother and a father."

I marinated on Brendan's words. "Do you want to get married?"

Brendan gasped, "Yes...you know I do! And we can make this work out!" Brendan held me for a long time. Although I felt safe and secure in his arms, making a decision to marry out of pressure and necessity was unsettling.

"I want to do this the right way," Brendan said. "I want fond memories for our future, so you'll have to wait for a proper proposal."

I wasn't the romantic type, and it seemed silly, but it was important to him, so I went along. I had never fantasized about white wedding gowns or wedding rings. I grew up with the notion embedded in my brain that marriage was a death sentence for the woman. Once married, we became old housewives that washed dishes, hung out the laundry, and catered to husbands who would become either controlling, unfaithful, or boring—and sometimes, all of the above. My father, though I loved him very much, was a philanderer. He eventually left my mother, even though she had done everything in her power to please him. All my life, I had just one dream, a dream that seemed so close just a few months ago. Now, I was turning my back on it and choosing to walk down another path. The fork in the road that wrestled with my heart no longer had my head turning this way and that, agonizing about which direction to take. I surrendered to providence and allowed my footsteps to lead me away from that dream.

49

PARADISE CITY

Three days later, during lunch, Brendan and I headed to the coast. He didn't say much. "It's a surprise, you'll see."

Driving west on MacArthur, we took a left on Pacific Coast Highway to an upscale residential area known as Corona Del Mar. At the botanical gardens, we turned right and drove four blocks to a property located on the first block from the grassy bluff just above the beach and parked the car on a shady street lined with mature trees. The custom-built homes in this area were spectacular, but the house that stood out as the most unique was the one Brendan and I approached.

It was a modern home that incorporated wood, stone, brick, and greenery for warmth and texture. In contrast, polished concrete, glass, and steel gave the home an industrial edge. The architect had created a perfect marriage between industrial sleek and wine-country rustic. It appeared to be newly built with fresh landscaping, and it stood out as the slick new kid on the block, situated on the corner next to a Tuscan style home.

"What is this, Brendan?"

"It's a special project I've been working on for a long time now."

The front entry was secluded, concealed by a ten-foot-tall wood fence made of four-inch horizontal teak wood slats. Passing through the front gate, we entered an intimate shade garden decorated with miniature Japanese maple trees, Japanese boxwood, baby's tears, white calla lilies, and horsetail reed. A stacked rock sculpture was nestled within the foliage, and water dripped from the top.

"This is beautiful. And the private entry is really nice," I complimented.

"I don't like solicitors," Brendan said. "It helps to keep them out."

"Is this your house?"

"We'll get to that. Check this out."

We passed through a large mahogany door with panels of obscured glass.

The interior was equally stunning. To the right, a floating staircase of walnut planks led to the upper floors, and to the right, a linear fireplace was situated aside a casual dining area. Beyond that was a large kitchen with natural walnut cabinets and professional quality stainless appliances, uncommon even in new homes in the early 1990s. The entire kitchen and dining room walls were wrapped with the same historic brick as the exterior. "These bricks were salvaged from an old factory outside New Orleans." Brendan conveyed. "When you use authentic bricks like this, you create an original custom design. You won't find many houses with bricks like this." I was in awe of the beautiful historic bricks. They were undeniably distinctive and filled the space with character and texture.

The layout was open with plenty of space. A classic black baby grand piano graced the open area. But what made this great room most impressive was that it stretched up two levels, boasting a thirty-foot ceiling with a glass elevator situated towards the entry of the living space. My eyes traveled here and there, gazing at each detail as I sank deeper into the mystery of it all.

The remaining first level housed a three-car garage, a guest room, and a full bath accessible through a wide threshold from the kitchen.

From the dining area, two triple-paned, double French doors led out to a quaint courtyard containing a primitive Asian-influenced water feature. A flagstone footpath with baby's tears growing in-between meandered through plant beddings; and on the far side lay a rustic kitchen garden of herbs and edible flowers.

The master suite, located on the second level, was accessible through a study. A see-through linear fireplace divided the master suite from master bath. I imagined how luxurious it would be to relax in a warm bath aside a flickering hearth.

The third floor housed two bedrooms with the remaining area dedicated to entertainment. The elevator divided the space between a large media center and a semi-formal dining area. The beautiful bowed plate glass window that I admired from outside was now revealing its interior perspective. The entire southwest wall consisted of floor-to-ceiling plate glass, offering unobstructed panoramic views of the Pacific Ocean. It was breathtaking.

I had never seen a home as magnificent as this modern mini mansion. "Brendan, this house is amazing."

Brendan, himself, was marveling at the dwelling. "I'm glad you like it. I bought the property three years ago and worked on the design with a buddy who's an architect. It was a work in progress for a long time, but when you and I stopped seeing each other for those long six months, I decided to finish it."

"This is yours?"

"Every square foot. There's a wine cellar, too, that you haven't seen yet—and there *is* something else."

We boarded the elevator and went to the roof, which looked like a large empty lot surrounded by a six-foot wall, excluding the ocean-facing wall, which was mostly Plexiglas. Over fifty percent of the rooftop was covered with slanted horizontal panels elevated a few inches above the wall. I pointed to a panel. "What are these?"

"These are solar panels. You will never again have to be cold in the winter. And you'll be comfortable every summer. You have to use your imagination, but this area can be a rooftop garden or anything else you want it to be. With the elevator, we could put small trees up here in this sunny section—lemon trees, orange trees--but I was thinking underneath these panels, a racecourse for big wheels or tricycles. We could design a track up here with old tires around the corners for bumpers, paint the walls with Grand Prix flags..." Brendan's imagination was running away with the prospect of his new family bringing life to this house. He looked at me lovingly. "I want this to be our house, together."

Speechless, I looked up at Brendan. His eyes traveled adoringly across of my face. From his pocket, he pulled out a gold twist tie, the kind that goes on cellophane gift bags. I watched as he skillfully made a ring out of it with a bow at the top.

"Margee, my love for you started to grow a month after I met you, because that's when I started to get to know you, and the more I get to know you, the more I love you. And with our baby, you've made me the happiest man alive. If you marry me, I promise to do everything I can to make you happy every day. I'll take care of you and our family forever."

I'm not a romantic person. It had to be my pregnant hormones in overdrive as emotional tears flowed on automatic.

"Will you marry me?"

It took a few moments before I could speak. "Yes," I answered, wiping away my tears.

"I thought it would be fun to go ring shopping together, so you can pick out what you want. But in the meantime..." He placed the twist tie on my finger.

In the distance, I could see what appeared to be the apparition of Catalina Island in the hush of the great gray Pacific, and a deep rush of peace surged through my body.

50

6TH AVENUE HEARTACHE

When I told Trevor and Greg that I was pregnant and that Brendan and I were getting married, I received two different reactions. Trevor went silent, but Greg was very encouraging. "That's great news! Congratulations! We'll have a baby Scarlet White. Lots of people have kids and still play in a band. I hope you're not thinking about quitting." Greg looked at Trevor for support. "Right, Trevor?...Trev?"

"Oh, yeah," Trevor responded after he snapped out of deep thought. "We should keep going, like Greg says."

Greg departed, leaving me alone with Trevor. I could feel his piercing eyes. "How far along are you?"

"Look, I know what you're thinking, and this baby is not yours, Trevor. I was nowhere near you when this baby was conceived. Besides, we used protection. Remember?"

"This isn't what you wanted, Margee, is it? You wanted a record deal more than anything. And we can do it. Besides, he's not like you."

"What? *You* don't know him."

"I do know him."

"What do you mean?"

"I mean...I know guys like him. I just don't think you and him match up. I think you had a real bad experience this past year with the Vixen, and with Randy and Mike leaving the band—"

"Trevor, you don't understand—"

"But why do you have to get married? Just two months ago you had no intention of marrying him."

"You have to understand, Trevor. A baby needs a lot of things—stability, security, a proper education, wholesome surroundings..."

"Right, and you could give this baby all that. He pays child support, and you continue with your plan, your life's work."

"Trevor, that's not the kind of mother I want to be for this baby, putting him in daycare all day while I work a day job, then leave him with a babysitter, so I can play gigs in dive bars and grungy nightclubs—"

"But Brendan could pay for all that. He could pay for you to stay home with the baby during the day. And at night he could, *and should*, take care of the baby. And it won't be grungy nightclubs forever."

"You don't get it, Trevor. This is Brendan's baby, and I want a loving father for this baby. And Brendan is a good man. He's a successful man. And he loves me. Besides, I'm tired of chasing after this fantasy. Things happen for a reason Trevor. This is real."

"You're over-thinking all this. And now you're taking the easy way out."

"Easy? Do you think this is easy for me? Look, I'm having a difficult time with this conversation. I don't have the energy anymore. I'm tired. I'm tired all the time now..."

"Do you love him?"

I hesitated for a second. "Yes...I do. But it's not about me. Everything has changed."

Trevor's demeanor exuded deep disappointment. Quietly, he surrendered. "Okay...you've made your decision, and I can see nothing is going to change your mind." He quickly departed and left me with a most confused and unsettled feeling.

Greg, Trevor, and I decided to take some time off. I knew that the right thing to do was cut all ties with Trevor now. So I pretended that I would return one day, but I knew I never would. It was better this way. To say goodbye, to say it was completely over, was too painful.

51

M!SSUNDAZTOOD

"My parents are nice people," Brendan explained, "but very traditional. You get married first, and then you have children. Anyway, I think it would be easier on them if we don't mention the baby just yet."

Brendan and I made plans to fly up to Connecticut to meet his parents right away, before the baby started to show. They would be celebrating their 40th anniversary, and it would give me the opportunity to meet the rest of the family as well.

Relieved by Brendan's suggestion, I also thought it best not to mention the engagement. A sudden announcement of Brendan's engagement to a woman the Knights had never met could very well put a damper on what was supposed to be a cheerful celebration for Mr. and Mrs. Knight. It could also arouse speculation about the pregnancy. So Brendan and I agreed that this initial meeting would serve as an introduction between the parents and me—a "just getting to know you" meeting so to speak—before we broke the news of the engagement down the road.

Brendan, an only son with two younger sisters, grew up in Connecticut on the Gold Coast. From what little I knew about Brendan's parents, I gathered they were well off. English immigrants, the Knights had relocated to the States when Brendan was two. Brendan's father decided to move his corporate headquarters to New York after merging with a company located in Manhattan.

My upbringing was in complete contrast to Brendan's. We were a family of six raised in a three-bedroom matchbox house, and our family shared one bathroom. Brendan had told me that he grew up in a big house, but this wasn't a house. It was a multi-million-dollar estate.

We entered the property through a large, double wrought-iron gate surrounded by old trees. The mansion was picturesque like an English manor partially grown over with ivy. We rounded a circular brick driveway with a large fountain in the center and parked.

Brendan's parents greeted us and seemed very polite. His mother was attractive, slender, and fit. She was dressed in white slacks, a gold silk blouse, and a navy blazer; her hair was up in a French twist. Carolyn Knight was a refined business-savvy woman who didn't smile very much. As an occupation, she sold real estate: multi-million dollar properties in the surrounding area, focusing on nouveau riche Wall Street clientele.

Similar in some ways, but in other ways quite different from Carolyn, Brendan's father came across as more down-to-earth and less discriminating. George was a tall man with beautiful blue eyes and a warm smile.

One other person greeted us, Yuki, an elderly Japanese woman of whom Brendan had often spoken. Yuki had been with the family since Brendan's father was a boy, and she currently maintained the tropical greenhouse garden where she grew primarily several varieties of orchids and ferns. Yuki had migrated with her husband from Japan to England as a new bride, and the young couple found employment with the Knight family. Yuki's husband had been in charge of the upkeep of the grounds and designing the gardens, while Yuki served solely as the nanny. Tragically, Yuki's husband died in a car accident just two years after they had begun service. The Knights had taken care of Yuki and vice-versa for two generations ever since. Yuki had also raised Brendan and been a live-in grandmother to Brendan's sisters.

Yuki's eyes turned misty as she bowed repeatedly, and she smiled broadly when we approached her. Brendan presented her with a gift, and she was enthralled. Although they didn't embrace, there was an indubitable bond spoken through their eyes, and it dawned on me that Brendan did have a real mother after all.

Following introductions, Brendan's mother showed us to our separate rooms where we settled in. Afterward, we returned downstairs for wine and appetizers, and I met Brendan's sister, Kate, and her husband, Rick. They had three children who were preoccupied with the Play Station. We conversed for a bit, but for the most part Brendan caught up with his parents regarding business matters, old acquaintances, and relatives. Just before dinner, Brendan's younger sister, Stacey, joined us.

Single and hearing impaired, Stacey was forthcoming, and I felt comfortable in her presence. Our conversation seemed to flow with ease. She was interested in relocating to California and asked about employment opportunities and the lifestyle. But what I didn't know about Brendan's family at this point was that every member was an Ivy League graduate.

During dinner, the topic of higher education came up at which point Carolyn directed the attention towards me. "What university did you attend, Margee?" I was caught off guard, not anticipating this question. I couldn't possibly tell her I had no desire to finish college, because I was going to be a rock star. The truth is: I judge how someone is going to react by my own reaction if I were put on the receiving end of the response. Whenever someone tells me they are in a band, I think, "Okay, just like billions of other dreamers with visions of grandeur—so what's your real job?" It really means nothing to me. Even if they are playing clubs on a regular basis, it still doesn't have a wow factor. But, when someone tells me, "I played in the studio with Steely Dan, or went on tour with Alicia Keys, or I performed in the Philharmonic orchestra", then I perk up. You've either made it or you haven't. And if you haven't, you're kidding yourself if you think someone is going to be impressed. You could be a mind-blowing performer, talented beyond light years, but if the person you're conversing with has never seem you on stage, you're nothing. Without a doubt, the eyes inside Mrs. Knight's brain would roll.

So I cleared my throat, and I lied a little. "I went to college for three years, but I couldn't afford to pay my tuition any longer, so I put my education on hold and started saving my money so I could finish down the road."

"Why don't you take out a loan to finish or apply for financial aid? Heavens, only one year left? Just be done with it. What were you studying?"

"Journalism—"

Brendan broke in. "Margee's been taking classes in desktop publishing and computer graphics on and off for several years now and has produced some nice marketing materials. She designed the brochure for our new line of urban biker sunglasses. Speaking of bikers, how's Uncle Marty doing? Did he ever buy that Harley?"

Just as if Brendan could read my mind, he changed the subject so the focus was no longer on my education, or the lack of it. I was rescued from the threat of humiliation, or so I thought, until everyone finished eating, and I noticed Mrs. Knight's eyes dart down at my plate in distaste. *What was she glaring at?* I thought.

I looked down at my plate, and then my eyes circled around the table, scanning everyone else's plate. They had all, including the children, placed their fork and knife together on their plates where the number four lies on the face of a clock. They had all left a small morsel of food as well. I, on the other hand, had finished every trace of food on my plate like a starving peasant. I may as well have licked my plate, as clean as I left it. I had been taught that it was a compliment to the cook to eat everything down to the last tidbit. However, in this case the chef was not dining with us. He was in the kitchen and would have no clue whose plate it was that would come back clean. But then again, perhaps he would.

I had also left my fork and knife sprawled apart, fork on the left, knife on the right—a low-class prostitute sitting with her legs spread. I couldn't help but to think that's probably what my fork and knife represented to Mrs. Knight. I could feel my face beginning to flush, followed by an urgency to fix it. As inconspicuously as possible, I raised my stealthy fingers to my plate, gently slid my fork over to the right side of my plate, placing it alongside my knife so it looked like everyone else's. I was aware that all eyes were upon me, and I felt the flush in my face deepen. Without thinking, I cleared my throat and placed my elbows on the table interlacing my fingers. Instantly, I realized that elbows on the table were rude, so I quickly returned my hands to my lap. A cocoon of discomfort swaddled me, and self-defeating thoughts were rambling through my head. *God, what an embarrassment. I'm so uncultured. I wish I were somewhere else right now. It sure is hot in here. I could use a stiff drink. Damn it, I'm pregnant. I can't drink... Jesus Christ I'm such a fucking loser...*

Suddenly, Brendan took his fork and gently slid it over to the other side of his plate so that it looked like mine before I corrected it! Brendan's sister, Stacey, started to giggle, and Brendan giggled too, like two mischievous children pushing the limits.

"So!" Mrs. Knight announced. "Shall we have brandy in the parlor?"

As we gathered in the parlor, Stacey handed me a brandy snifter containing a shallow pool of cognac. "Brendan tells me you like cognac. Try this." She lowered her voice and added, "It's over eighty years old."

Stacey informed everyone that she would be giving me a tour of the home. "Come with me, Margee. You don't want to hang around Brendan and Dad when they start talking about business. It can get a little boring unless you're into that sort of thing."

I pounced on Stacey's offer to separate from the rest of the family. What a shame that I was unable to drink this rare cognac. I took the smallest sip (or two), and decided to give the rest to Brendan.

Stacey proceeded to give me a tour of the mansion. We headed back to the dining room, passed through a butler's pantry, and entered a massive kitchen with black and white checkerboard marble tiles. Restored to its original glamour, the kitchen was flanked with high ceilings and a walk-in refrigerator large enough to hold floral arrangements and several platters for a large catered party. The chef, his assistant, and two house staff were cleaning up. The chef, from Manhattan, had been hired for the evening to prepare Mr. and Mrs. Knight's anniversary dinner. We complimented him and departed.

A wide threshold connected the kitchen to a split decagon conservatory. Four fifteen-foot palms surrounded the room, reaching upward to the semi-dome glass ceiling. A Chinese elm console supported a grand bouquet of orchids. Each botanical beauty was placed in an equally beautiful pot of blue and white Ming Dynasty porcelain. "This is my favorite room," Stacey said. "As you can see with all the healthy plants, it has Yuki's presence all around. This is where we'll have breakfast." Beyond the glass walls, several ancient oaks were illuminated by up-lights in the lawn.

Stacey's fondness of the home was deep-rooted as if she had lived in this house in a past life. I was fascinated with her stories of the former inhabitants and her in-depth knowledge of architecture and antiques. Due to her hearing impairment, her speech sounded different than most people's, but she was natural and comfortable in her skin. We continued up the stairs when she stopped by my room. "By the way," she said, "we have a ghost. But no need to worry, he pretty much stays in this room." She nodded her head at my door. "This one." She lowered her voice. "In the late 1800s, he died in this room. People who have stayed in here say that sometimes at night, they can hear him singing."

"Singing?" I asked.

"Yes—well, more like chirping. But he stays in the closet."

"Chirping."

"Yeah. He's a cricket." She smiled and nudged me.

"You had me spooked for a split second there, Stacey."

"Our house at Martha's Vineyard really is haunted. I could tell you some strange stories about that house."

"I love ghost stories, actually. So long as the ghost isn't in my room."

We continued to stroll through the mansion, and Stacey revealed that Brendan had always been rebellious, as was witnessed with the knife-and-fork shenanigan. "And somehow," Stacey said cocking her head, "he has always managed to get everything he has ever wanted in life. Either through persistence or patience or whatever—if he decides he wants something, it will be his sooner or later."

"Do you consider that to be a good or bad trait?" I questioned.

"You know, that's a good question. Most of the time it's good, I think. But once in a while, maybe not."

I came to learn over time that Stacey had a much closer relationship with Brendan than she did with Kate.

Stacey had often taken silent sideline pleasure in Mrs. Knight's disgruntlement over Brendan's defiance, playful or otherwise. As controlling as Mrs. Knight was, and as hard as she tried, she could not control Brendan and learned that she never would, which took me by surprise. Brendan had always come across as passive and easygoing in his interactions with me, encouraging me to make my own choices. We rarely had conflicts, and the few times that he felt adamant about having his way about something, I acquiesced without resentment.

52

GET WHAT YOU GIVE

woke up to my first dilemma: what to wear?

Before turning in, Mrs. Knight informed everyone that reservations had been made to play golf at the Lakeside Country Club and that breakfast would be served at 8:30 a.m. sharp.

I picked through my suitcase…*golf attire…what looks close to golf attire?* I had no idea when I packed for this trip that I would be playing golf with the Knights at the elite West Lake Country Club, and I was not looking forward to playing a game I had only ever watched for a few minutes on TV. Fortunately, I had brought a brand new pair of blue suede skateboard shoes. But everything else went downhill from there.

Already ten minutes late, I threw on my baseball cap, put my aviator sunglasses above the brim and rushed downstairs. I offered a cheerful, "good morning" when I entered the conservatory, and all heads turned to get an eyeful. Hauling band equipment combined with kickboxing classes had sculpted my five-foot-four, one-hundred and ten-pound body. With cut-off denim shorts and a tight tank top that revealed a bit of skin along my lower waistline, my physical features were now on display for the whole crew. I regretted not waking up earlier so I could have been seated first. Once settled in between Brendan and Stacey, she nudged me discretely and whispered, "You're going to be my new cool friend."

There was a slight overcast, and the grounds were vivid green from the midnight rain. A family of elder oaks with limbs spread wide dipped down, then up to sky to embrace the light. About fifty yards in the distance, a small canal ran through the property where a large willow tree stood, its fronds sweeping gracefully just inches above the water. About eighty yards beyond the canal was a wooden post fence where several young girls in equestrian uniforms were taking their horses out for a jaunt.

"What do you think?" Brendan asked breaking my spell.

"Oh...sorry," I sighed. "I was just taking it all in. I think it's the most beautiful backyard I've ever laid eyes on. I could sit in this room for hours on end and be thankful for every second."

Mr. Knight smiled at me sweetly.

I made my plea to Mrs. Knight, and I tried to talk her into letting me sit this one out. "I've never played golf before, but I'll make a great caddie."

However, Mrs. Knight would not take no for an answer. "Good heavens my dear, it's just a game. It's all in good fun. Try not to take it so seriously."

Truth be told, the Knights were ardent golfers, and most of them did take the game seriously. To make matters more interesting, Carolyn invited a special guest to tag along, Lisa Hollingsworth, another avid golfer who also just happened to be Brendan's high school sweetheart.

I learned much more about Lisa Hollingsworth a year later during one of Stacey's subsequent visits to California. Lisa and Brendan had dated through senior year in high school, then two more years, long distance, while Lisa attended Oxford to study law. Lisa came from a prominent family of prestigious professionals, business tycoons, and high-ranking political officials: her father was a judge, her uncle a senator, her brother a plastic surgeon to the rich and famous...

Brendan, in his youth, was initially swept away by Lisa, who possessed a bewitching knack for first impressions. And Carolyn had high hopes of uniting the Hollingsworth family with the Knights, so Brendan was fervently encouraged by his mother to foster the relationship. But as time passed, Brendan came to realize that Lisa had control issues spawned by her self-centered nature. This trait began to expose its fangs one too many times towards the end of Brendan and Lisa's relationship. She dictated, though in a genteel way, how Brendan should dress, behave, wear his hair... She criticized him for his sense of humor, his lack of proper etiquette, or anything else she deemed unacceptable. She even tried to convince Brendan to break ties with some of his best friends. In short, she didn't want Brendan for who he was.

Nonetheless, Lisa had her sights set on hooking him. She discussed wedding plans without a proposal. Yet, there was another problem Brendan could foresee. For a wife, he didn't want a career woman, much less a selfish career woman. In my own conversations with Brendan, he made it clear that he wanted a woman who didn't frown upon motherhood and raising children full time. But Lisa had made it clear that she was going to have a career. Later, in her desperation to snag Brendan into marriage, she claimed that she would be okay with staying home and raising the children, but Brendan continued to have reservations. Although his own mother had not raised him, Yuki was as good a mother as they come. She possessed all the qualities Brendan admired in a woman. She was compassionate, gentle, and courageous, with a strong spirit and unsurpassed character. She devoted her life towards raising Brendan's father, his siblings, and then Brendan. But when the girls were born, she had become too old to raise yet another child, and thus the job was handed down to a younger house staff member, Anna, while Yuki inherited the comfortable role as the second grandmother to the girls. Brendan wanted his future children to have a loving mother similar to Yuki. I had once asked Brendan if he resented his mother for choosing not to raise him herself.

"Absolutely not," Brendan expressed. "I'd be a mess if she raised me. Having Yuki raise me was the best gift my mother could give."

But Brendan could foresee that nannies like Yuki would cease to exist in our rapidly changing culture. Most modern-day nannies are strangers with a résumé, and parents could only hope their child would be in the hands of a person who would love and care for their child as if the child were their own—same as Yuki had loved and cared for Brendan. Brendan's instincts and common sense had led him to believe that the only person suitable to love and nurture his children would have to be their own mother, so long as she would embrace motherhood wholeheartedly and relish taking the job on a full-time basis. Lisa, as Brendan came to realize, was not only unlike Yuki, she was the extreme opposite.

In the end, Lisa Hollingsworth did not fulfill Brendan's expectations as a life partner and the future mother of his children. And when Brendan woke up, he broke up. Lisa became outraged and accused Brendan of leading her on and using her during her prime years. With these accusations, Lisa had felt that she could guilt Brendan back into a relationship. But when this tactic failed, Lisa gave it a break, though she never gave up. She went bouncing from one relationship to the next, never finding anyone who could meet Brendan's benchmark. So periodically, Lisa would drop in at family functions and behave adoringly towards Brendan in a futile effort to win him back. Though Brendan had lost interest in Lisa, Carolyn had not.

The second we stepped foot inside the Lakeside Country Club lobby, Lisa Hollingsworth rushed to Brendan and hugged him so tightly she nearly knocked him down. When Brendan introduced us, her eyes shifted down and up sizing up my ensemble. Her lips formed a smile. I reached out to shake her hand.

"Hi, Lisa, pleasure to meet you."

"Likewise."

Shaking her fingers felt awkward. Seemed odd that someone who practiced law didn't have a proper handshake.

Lisa immediately turned her focus to Mrs. Knight. Delighted to see each other, Carolyn and Lisa kissed cheek-to-cheek. It made me think of Sanjoy and how much I missed him. When we greeted, we also kissed cheek-to-cheek, except we would kick one heel up on the second kiss. This was our signature greeting, and it always seemed to make us giggle. I longed for Sanjoy's support right now. He would be giving Lisa the evil eye.

Lisa returned to Brendan, linked his arm with hers, and escorted him to the counter. I couldn't help but notice the expression on Stacey's face. She was clearly annoyed. I felt a strange pain in the center of my stomach—like someone had punched me in the gut—as I endured a shocking blow to my self-esteem.

Carolyn had prearranged the two teams. The members on Mrs. Knight's team were Lisa, Brendan, and Kate. And the members on Mr. Knight's team were Stacey, Rick, and me. As expected, I turned out to be a huge handicap for my team. Because Mr. Knight was the superior golfer amongst the group, I was placed on his team. Everyone else was relatively evenly matched. Although Mr. Knight was exceptional at golf, the others were not that far behind. In any case, I decided I would just do my best to wing it. Besides, I reasoned, *how hard could this be?*

But it was hard—just like most things we do for the very first time. My tee off sucked. I had a ferocious swing, if only it could connect with the ball. After two attempts, I finally hit the ball, but it went flying forty-five degrees into a cluster of trees. Lisa, taking great pleasure in my snafu, produced a complacent grin.

After the first three holes, our team was falling far behind until both teams agreed that Mr. Knight should tee off for me, and then I would handle the rest.

Like Mr. Knight, my father also loved golf. Because he was in the military, he had free access to a small golf course in Augusta, and he took advantage of that privilege.

Typically, any avid golfer would attest that miniature golf is nothing like golf, but when it comes to putting, I would have to insist that they are wrong. As a young girl, my father took me to every miniature golf course in the county and gave me explicit instructions on how to hold the putter as well as putting techniques, until I became good enough to get a hole in one nearly every time.

Of course, I didn't dare bring up my miniature golf magnificence to this crew. But by the tenth hole, as long as the golf ball was within fifteen yards of the hole, I managed just fine much to everyone's surprise. Due to my incompetence on the first three holes, I had left my team spirit trodden and far behind. Lisa and Mrs. Knight were noticeably smug with their team's reign, but by the twelfth hole, our team began creeping up from behind. It had been at least thirteen years since I played miniature golf, and I needed the first eight holes or so just to warm up.

Somewhere around the tenth hole, Brendan's game started to go south until the scores on both teams began to even out. After Brendan's third error, it was becoming obvious he was not making an honest effort. When one of his balls flew into the sand trap, he laughed, and Lisa gave him a stern look of disapproval. With one hand on her hip and her mouth hung open, she was unable to suppress her thoughts. "Brendan...What are you doing?"

"I'm just having one of those off days, I guess."

By the eighteenth hole, both teams were tied. And our team's success would depend on my last putt. I had to make a twenty-foot putt to win the game. I had this strange feeling I had been in this position before, minus the severe stress factor. Mr. Knight placed one hand on my shoulder, and his eyes pierced mine as if the pressure was not already immense. At that very moment, he reminded me so much of my father. He spoke, quietly, earnestly. "My dear, it all depends on you. You have to make this one, Margee."

My anxiety level was so extreme, I swore to myself that no one would ever talk me into playing golf again, *ever*. A heat wave surged through my body as beads of sweat rolled down the back of my neck and the sides of my face. I wondered—*How did I get here? How did my life end up here? I was supposed to be a fucking rock star. I should be nervous about performing in front of thousands of people, not playing golf at some ritzy country club in Connecticut for Christ's sake.* But as fate would have it, I was here, so I had to make the best of it. What choice did I have anyway?

I noticed from another putt made on this last hole that the landscape sloped just a tad, and I would have to compensate and putt in an arch in order make this shot. I approached my golf ball with consternation and positioned my putter. I drew in a deep breath, closed my eyes for two seconds, and released my breath slowly. As I exhaled, a strange peacefulness came over me, as if I had detached myself from this dimension and plunged into the realm of another world. It was like living in a dream. I opened my eyes, and I shuffled my feet into place. I looked at the hole, and back at the ball, and shuffled a second time. Finally, I gave the ball a hearty tap with a ten-degree arch. It seemed to roll forever. Those eight seconds felt like an eternity, and when the ball approached the hole, it began to roll ever so slowly. At the crest of the hole, the ball decided it was going to just rest on the very edge and settle there. At that split second, I imagined the ball having a face, laughing at me. I imagined the ball speaking to me, "Psych!" But mother nature was on my side. At that precise moment, a gust of wind like ancestral spirits watching over me gave that impudent ball one last little push. The ball teetered, and down it dropped.

My team exploded with cheer. I had never witnessed a lot this refined behave so wildly. Mr. Knight was roaring with laughter, dancing. I dropped to my knees, spread my arms wide, and looked up to the heavens. There *is* a God.

Another person on our rival team had also jumped for joy when my ball rolled in: Brendan.

Smoldering with resentment, Lisa Hollingsworth found her earliest opportunity to depart. This would be the last game of golf I would ever play and the last time I would ever see Lisa Hollingsworth.

53

BRONWYN ADIA KNIGHT

She laid quietly on my belly. I looked down at her for the first time to find two beautiful, light brown eyes gazing right back at me.

On May 23, 1992, Bronwyn was born.

Love, on a level that I had never known before, had shined its light upon me, and nothing else mattered except her. I nuzzled her feathery hair, inhaled her scent, and showered her with kisses. Holding her to my heart produced a chemical reaction, a deep swell of endorphin. Becoming a mother was a revelation. I now fully understood that the power of a mother's love is the most intense and euphoric form of love in the universe. It's a love that could only be felt by a mother for her child. From that day forward, all my priorities changed.

Three months later, Greg phoned me. He asked questions about Bronwyn, then opened the conversation up to the band. "So I met a guitarist who might be a good fit for the band. What should I tell him? Just wondering if you've given any thought about getting back into the studio any time in the near future?"

"Brendan's been traveling a lot, Greg. I'm not comfortable leaving her alone with a babysitter yet. Just taking things day-by-day for now."

Holding on to a measure of hope, Greg feigned optimism. "I understand. Hey, don't worry about it. I tell you what, take your time, and call us when you're ready."

Unlike before, when I imagined it ripping my heart in two to leave the band, I found this decision less difficult now, although bittersweet. I requested that the project be put on hold, indefinitely. It was easier this way. Much easier than saying goodbye and fully accepting that this was the official end of the Scarlet White project. I knew Trevor and Greg were not going to wait for me.

54

HEART OF THE MATTER

"Margee?"

I turned around to find Randy smiling at me as though nothing had happened between us.

It was a warm August day, Brendan and I, along with baby Bronwyn, had just finished watching Alturas perform at The Taste of Orange County and decided to eat some empanadas. As Brendan held a table with Bronwyn, I waited in line, when I heard someone call my name.

Randy and I had parted on such bad terms, I didn't know how to react. He had heard that I married Brendan, and oddly, the first thing Randy wanted to see was my ring. "That's it?" he scoffed.

"I picked the ring," I said. "I don't like big diamonds. Not my style." I shrugged.

"You should see the ring I bought for Dayna. It's two carats. People are blown away by the size of it."

Although the trend in diamonds was competitively big, a doorknob on my finger would have interfered with sports and guitar. I could never figure out why low-income couples would trade an African safari or a Mediterranean sailing adventure for a chunk of carbon. This encounter confirmed my sentiment that the size of the diamond was not relative to the husband's wealth. Randy, still unemployed, made a meager income making custom pool cues for his father's business part-time. Randy's comment left me feeling awkward. Not knowing how to respond, I changed the subject. "How *is* Dayna?"

"She turned out to be a controlling bitch. We broke up, and now she's dating some alcoholic jarhead. But, I got the ring back."

Randy had proved me right in my second sentiment in that the size of the diamond is not a measurement of love. Furthermore, the band Dayna set Randy up with never panned out. He asked, "Whatever happened with your friend, Lori? Did she get that record deal?"

"I really don't know. I assume so."

"You know," Randy said, "when I think back on the Vixen, something strange happened that night. It didn't add up. We got screwed, and to think that Lori—of all people—got signed by Geffen. She seemed like such a lost cause. Talk about making it without paying any dues. It should have been us."

"I know, but it's all in the past now."

It was apparent that over time, Randy had grown regretful. And how could he not? It wasn't just the time and money we invested; we were having the time of our lives. But at least I had a husband, a baby, and a beautiful home to call my own, while Randy had nothing to show for the years of his life that he had dedicated towards music. My heart went out to him.

"Randy, don't give up. You're the best guitarist I've ever known. It was such a privilege working with you."

Randy's face transitioned into a display of resignation as he completely relinquished the ill will that he had harbored towards me for the past year and a half. "You're not so bad yourself, Scarlet. Does this mean we can bury the axe?"

"Of course, Randy." I hugged him, and my heart felt lifted knowing we were okay now.

55

I'M JEALOUS

Brendan had promised that he'd be home early, which was becoming more infrequent lately. After cleaning the bottom half of the house, I decided to drive to the market to buy ingredients for braised short ribs. It was Brendan's favorite. The morning mist had faded, leaving pale lavender-gray clouds painted across the blue, when a familiar song on the radio drew me out of my reverie. Then it dawned on me. The song was one I had composed and sang many years ago. I hadn't heard the song since that fateful night at The Vixen. I pulled over as my heart began to thump and my breath grew heavy. Oddly, I continued to listen, enduring the tug-of-war between fascination and self-destruction.

In the months to follow, Lori's album, *Broken Wing*, took off. Two of my songs crossed over to several genres and were played on three radio stations. Brendan, sensitive to my grief, was careful to always play CDs when we were in the car together. Though I tried hard to suppress it, feelings of humiliation and betrayal, as well as the loss of a lifelong dream, continued to stab at my soul like a searing dagger that burned in my memory like it had all happened just yesterday.

Later that winter, Brendan, Bronwyn, and I were visiting the neighbors, Marcella and Sean, along with two other couples. Marcella had prepared enchiladas, and everyone was having a pleasant time, when one of the guests blurted, "The Grammy's are on right now." Marcella turned the television on, and no more than five minutes passed when Tunnel Love took the stage.

In her South American accent, Marcella commented. "Okay, you know what, I *really* like that esong. This girl is such a good esong writer. I'm telling you she is going to be the next big thing."

When I started my new life as a wife and mother, I didn't share my past with anyone. As far as they knew, I met Brendan when I worked at Urban Perspective as a graphic designer. Revealing information about my musical life would spark inquiries, and inquiries would place me in a position of having to recall painful memories of failure. I watched Lori perform with a green heart, swollen with envy. Tunnel Love took the Grammy for best new album, and when Lori got up to accept the award, I caught a glimpse of a familiar person in her entourage, Sanjoy, in all his glory, hobnobbing with the rich and famous, smiling ear-to-ear, fraternizing with the enemy. He gave Lori an adoring kiss on her cheek. Another douse of poison surged through me. Brendan, sensitive to my torment, made an excuse to cut the evening short. And we walked home in silence.

56

WITH ARMS WIDE OPEN

"Mommy, you love Jude more than me."

She wasn't whining or fishing for attention. She was expressing her true feelings.

"I love you both the same. Jude is a baby. That's why I carry him. I used to carry you all the time too."

Bronwyn started to wiggle away from me when she was old enough to walk. She had never cared for too much physical affection, but Jude was just the opposite. He loved being smothered with hugs and kisses. I continued to talk to her. "You know when Mommy brushes your hair and scratches your back, or when Mommy takes naps with you, and I put my arm around you...that's the same as hugs and kisses. That's the same as carrying you."

Bronwyn's eyes widened. "Mommy! Brush my hair, please!"

As I brushed her hair gently in front of the mirror, I giggled inside. Her eyes were rolling into her head as she wallowed in a river of bliss. I inhaled the sweet scent of her hair and kissed the top of her head.

On February 16, 1995, Jude Alexander was born. Just like Bronwyn, he was immediately placed on my belly, and when his eyes finally met mine, I saw they were crystal blue like pools of glacier waters. He was beautiful, and I fell in love all over again.

Jude was easy going and smiled his entire waking hours. He woke in his crib cooing, and he called out for me in his own baby language. I could hear him through the baby monitor. We were like mother monkey and baby monkey, always together, clinging to each other, and I was in heaven. Because we decided he was to be our last baby, I carried him often. Truth be told, I never wanted to put him down. I waited patiently for him to wake up from his nap so I could begin the cycle all over again—feed him, play with him, rock him to sleep. I had never in my life experienced anything as fulfilling and rewarding as the time I spent loving and caring for my babies. Some moments felt transcendental: snap shots of nirvana. But, this was also an era of contrasts. As with many older siblings who received a lot of attention those first years, it was a difficult time for Bronwyn. And she began to demand my attention without pause.

57

WISH YOU WERE HERE

"Wow baby, what a big poopy!" I exclaimed.

It was one of those huge ones. The kind that squished almost out of the diaper all the way up Jude's back and took five diaper wipes to clean.

Unable to suppress her curiosity, Bronwyn, who was having her dinner, jumped out of her seat to take a look, when the combination of the vegetables in her mouth and the look and smell of the diaper were more than she could stomach. A fountain of puke spewed from her mouth. "Bronwyn, sit down!" I blurted. But I should have instructed her to go to the bathroom. "No, Bronwyn, I mean go to the bathroom and throw up in the toilet!"

Bronwyn redirected herself to the toilet, as the trail continued. I finished cleaning Jude and placed my bottomless baby in his playpen then proceeded to clean the trail of vomit before Bronwyn would have a chance to track it to other areas of the house. I threw Bronwyn's clothes into the washing machine and got her washed and dressed. When I returned to the playpen to put a diaper on Jude, he greeted me with the sweetest smile. Even with a pacifier in his mouth, he had the most cheerful smiling eyes. But something brought my focus south. Jude had sprung a leak, completely soaking his playpen. Quickly, I washed the playpen mat in the side yard and left it to dry. Meanwhile, the carrots on the stove had completely burned black to the pot. "Damn it!" I cursed.

Fortunately, the remaining dinner was salvaged: Paul Prudhomme's Cajun meatloaf with peas, garlic mashed potatoes, with a tossed salad, all paired with a nice Zinfandel. Thirty minutes later, the table was set, the kids were fed, the toys were picked up, the hands were cleaned, the teeth were brushed, the bedtime stories were read, the bedtime songs were sung, the backs were scratched, and the hugs and kisses were exchanged. I never got around to making those phone calls, watering the plants, or finishing the laundry, and poor Duncan was still meowing for me to feed him, so I filled his food and water bowl. Finally, it was time to take care of me. I poured myself a fat glass of wine.

With the birth of Jude, my life changed exponentially. The demands I faced day-to-day were unrelenting as my life began to resemble the life of a billion other mothers, and at times, I felt like a faceless clone.

Days like this wiped me out. Exhaustion to the Nth degree consumed me. For energy, I resorted to two shots of espresso—one in the morning and one at noon. And to wind me down, I drank two...sometimes four glasses of wine in the evening, several days a week. But another factor weakened my spirit. I was lonely for companionship on an adult level as Brendan's job became more demanding, spending most of his time at the office and very little time at home.

I missed Sanjoy. I missed him terribly, but his friendship with Lori was impossible for me to accept. When he called, I made excuses about how swamped I was. I punished him, and he was clueless why.

I became poisoned by my jealousy of Lori, which ate away at my soul each time she popped into my head. And she popped into my head often. When I stood in line at the grocers, at least two magazines featured her on the front cover. Sometimes her attention was negative. Nevertheless, she received endless attention.

As time passed, I began to lose myself. My longing to connect with someone on a deeper level was never satisfied. I was trapped in this life I created, never going anywhere, yet growing older. And often times, too many times, I dreamed about Trevor. But those thoughts only seemed to make my longing and loneliness more pronounced.

This became my blue phase. It became the decade of loneliness, waiting for Brendan to come home. As the years passed, Brendan's work hours and travels increased, and I rarely saw him. Rather than complain, I became distant and my love for him turned listless.

58

COMPLICATED

"Bronwyn, a C in History? You made A's on all your quizzes and tests. How did this happen?" My eyes scanned the rest of her trimester report. "Four C's, and one B? Bronwyn! All because you didn't turn in any homework! Why Bronwyn?"

She shrugged as she rested her temple in her palm at the dinner table, pushing her peas around her plate.

"Bronwyn? Can you explain?"

"I don't understand why I need to do homework if I'm making A's on all my tests! It's busy work for retards, and it's not fair that someone with a higher level of intelligence such as myself has to do all that busy work just because the retards need it!"

At twelve, Bronwyn had sprouted up. She stood nearly as tall as me and was a full-fledged tomboy. She and Jude were academically advanced and placed in accelerated classes in private schools, acing on exams and standardized testing with little effort. But at thirteen, Bronwyn went from making all A's to C's when she decided that school work was to be done only while at school, not at home. By fourteen, I was looking up at her. She was stunning, with long reddish-brown hair down to her hips. But along with her good looks came an attitude and a will that could not be broken or even bent. She stood with her chest out and shoulders back like an anime character, and she was stubborn to the bone.

On the weekend, half a dozen or more boys were in and out of our garage tweaking or upgrading their skateboards, preparing to ride along the boardwalk. One summer while my dad was visiting, I expressed my uncertainty with Bronwyn's friends all being boys. My father responded, "I once knew a pretty young girl who rode skateboards, played guitar, and hung out with all the boys too. Man, that girl used to laugh to the top of her lungs. Whatever happened to that girl?"

On several occasions, I noticed an older boy who lived across the street gawking at Bronwyn on her way home from school. I shared my vexation with Brendan. "He's at least twenty-one! One day I'm going to run over there and punch his stars out."

Bronwyn and Brendan occasionally engaged in horseplay in which Brendan took a beating from her. "I feel sorry for anyone who lays a hand on Bronwyn. She can take care of herself," Brendan assured me.

But the thing that unhinged me the most when it came to Bronwyn was her idol. Ironically, a life-size poster of Lourdes Love hung comfortably on Bronwyn's bedroom wall. Forgiveness was out of the question, but even if I wanted to forget, each time I entered Bronwyn's room, Lori seemed to be staring at me saying, "Now look who's rich and famous, and your daughter loves me more than you."

As the years passed, I became infected by my jealousy of Lori, and I dwelled on my failure to be something of value, as I realized that I had accomplished nothing of what I considered real significance in my life. My wealth had come through marriage rather than my own efforts. But Lori's wealth was her own. I tried my best to be a good mother, but I wasn't sure if I was succeeding even at that as Bronwyn continued to put me to the test. I blamed myself for Bronwyn's misgivings and bad behavior.

One evening at dinner, I was pleasantly surprised when Bronwyn inquired about my guitar, which I had stored in the guest room closet along with my old Mesa Boogie amp. "Mom, whose guitar is in the guest room closet?"

"That's my guitar."

"Were you in a band?"

"I was...for a long time," I bragged. " I played around the same time that Lourdes Love was coming up...before she got signed with Geffen."

"Were you anywhere near as good as Lourdes Love?"

"I bet Mom was better than Lourdes Love!" Jude chimed in.

"If Mom were better than Lourdes Love," Bronwyn disputed, "then *Mom* would be a rock star, not just some random boring housewife, nube."

"Shush, Bronwyn!" I scolded. "Don't speak to him like that. What's the matter with you? Go to your room until you can decide to be nice!"

Bronwyn continued to test my limits. Knowing what she was capable of and seeing her grades fall put a great damper on our relationship. I found myself continually nagging her. I banned her from computers and gaming and took her cell phone away. She would scream at me, run to her room, and slam the door. A few minutes would pass, and she would return to badger me without pause. "Why are you so unfair? You're just like those crazy Asian tiger moms!" She followed me around the house draining me of every ounce of patience and energy. "All the other kids are making C's, and their parents let them game for hours!"

At times, she would get the best of me. I'd lose it and find myself screaming at her. And many times, I would resort to downing a glass of wine to soothe my nerves.

As a teenager, Bronwyn's obstinance never subsided, and she bailed out challenges for me on a daily basis. Little did I know that these battles with Bronwyn were relatively trivial. As my mother liked to say, "This is everyday teenager stuff, Moggie." And she was right—it was everyday teenager stuff compared to the bomb that was about to drop on my future.

59

ISLAND IN THE SUN

It was early spring of 2004 when Brendan made the announcement. "Margee, we are going to Cancun!" Brendan became an equal partner with Mark Zander, CEO at Urban Perspective, and the company became Zander Knight. They expanded from surf accessories to clothing, shoes, and skateboards. Brendan was working longer hours and traveling more often, and it had been two years since our last family vacation together.

Mid-December of 2004, the family had three days of calm paradise in Cancun and the Mayan Riviera. After two days on the beach swimming, kayaking, and fishing, we visited the ancient archeological site of Chichen Itza. I tried to imagine what life was like in the year 800, when human civilization was still in its budding stage, as I meandered through this breathtaking Mayan ruin. To imagine going back that far was mind boggling, and having the opportunity to view this structure with its remains so well intact was pure fascination for me.

Just before sunset, we drove to the beach to take a short hike and stumbled upon a secluded bay with breathtaking vistas.

"There's a picnic table up there." Brendan pointed to a grassy area under some trees. So we decided to sit and soak in the spectacular fire-orange sunset and watch the kids in the distance make a sand castle to house some unsuspecting hermit crabs. Just moments after we were seated, I was taken off guard when an eager Mexican strolled up and passed out handwritten menus. I had assumed that the picnic tables were public. The establishment, which was several yards away, appeared to be more like a dwelling than a restaurant, but Brendan didn't give it a second thought. "Oysters on the half shell sounds good. Do you want something?"

"No thanks. I'll just have a beer."

60

HOW TO SAVE A LIFE

marveled at the army of hermit crabs making tracks in the freshly raked sand in our beach front veranda as I sipped my coffee. It was already mid-morning, and I was anxious to begin our snorkeling excursion at Shipwreck Reef. I downed the last drop and went upstairs to give Brendan a nudge. "Brendan, we should be going soon. The reef might get crowded later in the afternoon."

Brendan lay face up with his eyes shut, exactly the same as when I left him an hour ago. "I don't feel good."

I placed my palm on his forehead. He was on fire.

By noon his condition escalated. He began to vomit uncontrollably, and by 6:00 p.m. his temperature rose to one-hundred and four, and he began to experience severe dysentery. I drove him to the hospital, and the doctor strongly advised us to return home to seek medical attention. Early the following morning, we caught the first flight back to Orange County. Brendan was in such a severe state of exhaustion, I could barely keep him awake to drink water. As soon as our flight arrived at John Wayne Airport, I drove him to the emergency room.

After intravenous hydration, Brendan's condition stabilized, and he was transferred to South Coast Hospital, where he was diagnosed with food poisoning: Vibrio Vulnificus, a bacterium found in oysters, isolated to those species found in warmer climates. He was administered antibiotics and missed nearly three weeks of work. When he gained enough strength to return, he carried the weight of the world on his shoulders at Zander Knight for the next year.

61

SKINNY LOVE

By winter, company growth had exploded for Zander Knight. Along with it came rigorous work hours for Brendan, including most weekends. In the evenings, he returned home exhausted and went straight to bed. He no longer woke at 5:30 for his morning jog as had been his usual routine prior to acquiring food poisoning. I started to notice a decline in his appetite and made mention of it. "Brendan, you barely touched your dinner tonight."

"I'm sorry, Margee. Work is really stressful right now. Once we hire two new managers, I'll be able to relax, but I can't drop the ball right now."

Months passed with providence refusing to relinquish Brendan from his burden, and his health continued to decline. I noticed significant weight loss, and his long-lost glowing complexion began to take on a yellow hue. Early spring, my mother moved in, helping me with household chores and meals, and life became somewhat easier. But I was deeply concerned about Brendan and urged him to see the doctor.

He finally acquiesced with a condition: "Okay, but first let me close on the Hiro contract and make one more visit to the manufacturing plant in Singapore." He continued to charge on until he collapsed late spring.

62

MY IMMORTAL

I sat anxiously in the waiting room, when Dr. Karnani approached and invited me into her office. "Mrs. Knight, here's where we stand. The images and test results are conclusive for liver cancer. At this stage, Brendan's liver has degenerated over sixty percent. The bigger issue is that the cancer has spread to his pancreas and stomach. We do have some options. You could choose treatment; however…"

The sound of Dr. Karnani's words faded into muddled background noise, as the message became more and more apparent that Brendan's illness was terminal. Because the cancer had spread to his pancreas and stomach, a liver transplant was not an option. He was not going to survive it. "How long does he have?" I asked.

"Three to six weeks. I'm very sorry Mrs. Knight."

A different type of sorrow rained down on me unlike any sorrow I had ever known.

I woke up in the morning with a few seconds of thinking it was all just a bad dream, and then reality struck like a viper and spread its venom through every cell of my being. There were times I wished I could just fall asleep and never wake up. But I knew that I needed to be strong for my family. As stoic as I pretended to be, so many emotions and thoughts saturated my mind. Selfishly, I became angry. I had been cheated again, but this time, on a much higher level. And this level made the first seem insignificant, because now fate was taking my husband—the father of our children—the man I was supposed to grow old with. My vision of Brendan walking on the beach with me in the last season of our lives, hand-in-hand, took on a different image as I saw him dematerialize, leaving me to walk alone. Between the anger and sorrow came deep sympathy for Brendan. He would never see the kids marry or even graduate. He would never have a chance to make up for all the years lost. His words were always the same. "Just a few more years, Margee, and I will be able to spend more time with you and the kids." But now that day would never come.

I cared for Brendan day and night, with help from the kids and my mother. Most days I would lie in bed with him, and we reminisced about the kids and when we met. "Remember when you made that long putt and won the golf game during my parents' 40th anniversary?" Brendan asked.

"How could I forget?"

"The way you shuffled your feet just before your putt. It was really cute. Your feet shuffled first, and then your hips would follow. You were the weekend entertainment for Dad."

I chuckled.

"You know," Brendan continued, "I was desperate to have you, Margee. I wanted to marry you more than I've ever wanted anything in my life. I don't think there was anything in my life that I wasn't able to get, and for a while there, I thought I wasn't going to get you. I'm so lucky to have had you as a wife. And the kids are lucky to have you as a mother."

"Brendan, you'll always be here in my heart. You'll be in Bronwyn and Jude's heart always and every day. In a strange way, we're lucky. We're lucky to have this opportunity to share how much we love each other and to remember all those special moments and memories."

For the next two weeks, Brendan and I continued to talk, laugh, and cry.

On August third, Brendan's pain reached its zenith. As the morphine entered his bloodstream, his pain subsided to a calm. He gazed into my eyes.

"Margee, did you have a happy life with me?"

"Brendan, why would you ask me that? Of course I've had a happy life."

Then Brendan seemed to become incoherent and rambled on with apologies. "I'm so sorry, Margee. I'm sorry you didn't live your dream. I'm sorry I took your dream away from you. I should have spent more time with you and the kids. I only hope you don't have regrets..."

Eventually, Brendan faded into a deep sleep, and his body began to shut down. I couldn't hold it in any longer. In between a barrage of tears, through a swollen throat and a breaking heart, all I could say was, "Brendan. It's okay. I would do it all over again. I wouldn't change anything. I love you, Brendan. I will always love you. It's okay to let go now Brendan. Let go..."

Brendan surrendered to his final moments of life—a faint ember to smoke, as he fell into an eternal sleep.

We had such little time to prepare. The children had lost their hero, and I, my knight in shining armor. I was devastated beyond repair, and so I took pills and I slept, and when I woke up, I took the pills again.

63

LITTLE WING

The glaring sun came crashing through my eyelids as I began to stir. I could discern activity in my room. I rolled over and opened my eyes to a squint, and I noticed my mother scrambling around my room. She brought clothes out of my closet. I placed my forearm over my eyes to shut out the light. Nearly two weeks had elapsed since Brendan's passing.

"Time to wake up, Moggie," my mother said in a semi-cheerful voice. "Wake up and come take a walk with me. Let's go to beach now."

"Not today, Mom."

"Yes, today, Moggie. What about Bronwyn and Jude? They can't lose Daddy and Mommy. You have to get out of bed. Put nice clothes on. You have to be Mommy and Daddy now. I stay if you get up. But if you sleep every day, I leaving, because I not helping you be this way. No good to sleep every day, Moggie. Bronwyn and Jude sad too. Time to wake up now."

"It's too soon, Mom."

"No, not too soon. You get up today, Moggie. Bad thing happen. Bad thing happen all the time in many people life. But still there is life to live. You have to be strong. Bronwyn and Jude have to go to school. They get up, they get dressed, so Mommy can do too."

I knew I would not be able to fight my mother today. I sighed and said, "Okay, Mom, I'll get up."

So I got up, and rather than walk, I ran. And I ran every day from that day on.

64

DROPS OF JUPITER

When the news had been delivered to Bronwyn and Jude that their father was terminally ill, they processed the information differently. Jude cried, but Bronwyn became reclusive. When Brendan passed away, Jude cried again, but Bronwyn became angry.

"He should have been around more!" she would snap, and there were no tears, or at least no tears in my presence. Bronwyn, now a high school Sophomore, had been a whiz at math so long as she put forth a little effort. To my dismay, her math grade dropped down to a D. One evening, she didn't come home from school for hours and would not answer her cell phone when I called. I became frantic. She was supposed to be home by sunset, and it had been dark out for over two hours. I called all her friends and eventually found out that she had been invited to a party with her volleyball team. But she never bothered to tell me. I was livid, I railed on her, and she screamed at me, "I hate you!" Those words pounded me like a sledgehammer. I was crushed.

One evening she announced that she was going to experiment with smoking pot. I decided that I just couldn't fight her anymore. She had taken all the fight out of me. As dusk fell into darkness, I sat in my bath and polished off a bottle of Opus One that Brendan and I were supposed to share on our 20*th* anniversary. I stared at the water that dripped from my tub faucet. I was losing her, and it was killing me.

65

I'LL FOLLOW YOU INTO THE DARK

t was 7:00 a.m., and she stared at her bowl of cereal. She was still in her zombie mode, too early for her to snap into the daily groove just yet.

"Would you like a cup of coffee?" I asked.

She looked at me, dazed and confused. It took a moment for her to comprehend. How could *I*, the nutrition nazi, offer her a cup of coffee?

"Sure," she said.

I poured her half a cup of coffee with half a cup of organic milk and added two teaspoons of Okinawan raw sugar. She sipped, and within minutes, she bloomed. While she was in this elevated state, I decided to talk to her.

"Bronwyn, I'm sorry I yelled at you the other night. It's just that I worry so much. Maybe too much. The thing is, until you have a child of your own, you will never know the depth of love I feel for you and Jude. But I don't want to fight you anymore. So if you really want to smoke pot, then I'll go get some, and we'll do it together. But I will never give up on you, and I will always expect you to do your best in school and in life. And when you don't come home, and refuse to answer your phone, and do poorly in school, it will break my heart again and again, and I'll get five more grey hairs and a few more wrinkles on my face. But I'm tired, Bronwyn. I know this past year has been really hard on you, but it's been hard on me too. It's been hard on all of us."

The following day, Bronwyn walked up to me as I washed dishes and put her arm around my shoulder. "Mom, I'm going to bring all my grades up. God forbid if you get more gray hairs and wrinkles." Weeks passed as she began to show signs of improvement, and our relationship finally seemed to be headed in a positive direction. But one night, to my surprise, she brought home a joint. "Mom, you don't have to get any pot. Justin next door gave me some."

I was flabbergasted. "Bronz, we don't know if this is safe. It could be tainted with chemicals."

"It's just pot, Mom."

My mother chimed in. "How about I testy? I smoke mayaku first and be mini pig."

Bronwyn laughed at Oba's self-sacrifice to test the pot and how she always called guinea pigs, mini pigs. But I finally convinced them that it would be better to let me buy the pot from a dispensary. "Besides, you really don't want to smoke it," I said, "The smoke will damage your lungs."

I was able to score a container of cannabis from Sanjoy. After the impact of Brendan's passing, Sanjoy had been kind and supportive, and I found my way back to him.

66

COMFORT EAGLE

The November winds subsided, and December arrived delivering its gentle rains—a nourishing welcome as they fell randomly, peacefully. Early one evening on a Saturday night while Jude was away at a sleepover, the three of us—Bronwyn, Oba, and I—made brownies out of a paste-like substance that reeked of concentrated pot. We each ate one brownie and parked ourselves in front of the plasma TV to watch *Toy Story*. After thirty minutes, Mom gave her assessment of the brownies. "I don't feel nothing. This mayaku no good," she said, shaking her head side-to-side in disappointment.

She must have repeated this five times, until halfway into the movie, the three of us realized we were plastered on the sofa on a starship to Mars.

"Do you still think the mayaku is no good, Mom?" I asked.

My mother stood up quickly, as though to get something, and immediately plopped back down. "Oh my Ga... This mayaku too good."

And the giggling began as my mother continued to say things that produced bouts of giggles. "I feel stuck. I feel like turtle. Like cool turtle...You know how turtle floats in ocean. Just hang around watchy all different fish swimmy...clown fish, blue fish, balloon fish..."

"What about a shark, Mom?"

"No! No sharky! Just fish make you feel happy kind of fish."

"What about an eel, Oba?"

"Sure! Eel look like zebra pokey head out of rock. Head go in, head go out and look around. That one happy."

Following tears of laughter and conversations about the anything and nothing, we passed out for twelve hours with pizza, barbeque sauce, ice cream, and chocolate cake stains on our faces and the places where we laid.

67

FEEL GOOD INC.

"Green tea? No Sapporo or sake?" Stacey relocated to Southern California four months after Brendan's passing when she was offered a position as director of engineering at a thriving company located in Irvine. I had not seen her since the funeral when she phoned me seeking company for dinner Friday evening. We settled on Kitayama, an upscale Japanese restaurant in Newport Beach.

"I haven't had a drink in three months, and I'm going to see how long I can keep it going."

"That's no fun!"

"I've done enough drinking in my life to last two lifetimes."

Stacey chuckled. "How are Bronwyn and Jude?"

"Bronwyn is doing much better in school now. Her grades are slowly getting better. Jude and I are taking karate classes together. We just got our orange belts."

"Didn't you take martial arts or Muay Thai before?"

"I did both. But I never got my black belt when I took karate the first time. I got all the way up to brown and quit, and I've always regretted not finishing."

"Good for you. That's great that you're taking the class with Jude. He's so cute and such a smart kid. He's going to be a heartbreaker just like Bronwyn. It's good to hear that she's back on track. But you know they're not normal teenagers unless they give you hard time. And so what's going on with Zander Knight?"

"I sold a portion of the company but held on to some stock, so I'm pretty set financially for the time being."

"For the time being and for years to come, I'm sure, unless you go on a spending spree, which I know you won't do."

Stacey's comment was accurate. I was sitting on a substantial chunk of money since I sold my half of the company. Brendan's hard work had paid off. Even if I lived comfortably for the next twenty years, including vacations abroad, I'd still be financially independent. I was considering investing in real estate or buying stock in Apple or Scholastic. A new book was due to hit the shelf soon that was the second in a series about a boy wizard called Harry Potter. Not to mention, Mr. and Mrs. Knight had offered to pay for the kids' education and basic needs. Mrs. Knight had finally came around and saw something good in me. Or it could be that she was falling for Bronwyn and Jude. Whatever the case, they were generous in their support.

Stacey and I continued to catch up with each other's current affairs.

"I have some bad news regarding Kate and Rick," Stacey revealed.

"Really? What's going on?"

"They're getting a divorce."

"What? I can't believe what I'm hearing. Kate and Rick seem so picture perfect."

"Between you and me, Kate isn't exactly the most honest person. She did some things that I don't think were fair to Rick."

"How so?" I asked.

"Where do I start? Okay, here's just one example. Rick was completely done with having kids after two, but Kate had to have three. So, she secretly poked holes in the condom pack with a needle so she could get pregnant without Rick knowing. I didn't think that was right. I mean, had the pregnancy been an accident, fine, but children should be a decision made by both the husband and wife together. Rick had scheduled himself to get a vasectomy, but he was just a wee bit too late. I think it was selfish of her. And I suspect Rick has wanted out of the marriage for quite some time. Kate's very controlling—like Mother."

Perplexed, I gazed at Stacey and began to ponder the information she had just delivered. "How did you find out that Kate poked holes in the condoms?"

"She told me."

"Did anyone else know about it?"

"What do you mean?"

"Who else did Kate tell...about poking holes in the condom packs? Were you the only person who knew about it?"

"Well, I don't know who else she would have told, but the night she told me, Brendan was there too. It was Brendan's 35th birthday. I remember the three of us were sitting by the fireplace outside by the pool. Kate had a little too much to drink, but I don't think anyone else knows about it. Why?"

For the rest of the night, I couldn't help wondering about Bronwyn's conception. I had been suffering adverse effects from the birth control pills. They weren't too serious, but Brendan convinced me to switch to condoms, insisting that taking the pill long-term may lead to more serious side effects. But after using condoms for only one month, I got pregnant. I had always thought that was odd. What were the chances? My pregnancy had been the catalyst for accepting Brendan's proposal. And the birth of Bronwyn changed my priorities completely. The day I found out about my pregnancy was the day my dream of a music career came to a halt, and the deal was sealed for Brendan.

68

THE ONLY EXCEPTION

struggled with the thought of letting go of Brendan's personal items, but over a year had passed since Brendan's death, and I felt perhaps the time had come to take small steps towards moving on with my life. Early on a Saturday morning after karate class, I finally mustered up the courage to at least go through his closet. I decided that if it came to the point where I could no longer do it, I'd just give it a rest and then go back to it down the road. I donated most of his clothes but kept several valuable and sentimental items, such as the suit he wore when we married and other various items that the kids cherished, including Brendan's watch, his favorite distressed brown bomber jacket, and a pair of platinum and gold cuff links.

My motivation continued through Sunday, so I decided to move forward and tackle the garage. Three years prior, Brendan had stored some file boxes that he had brought home from work. He placed them in the third garage on the wall adjacent to the washer and dryer.

Shortly after Urban Perspective expanded and became Zander Knight, more space was needed to accommodate twelve new hires, and these file boxes were taking up valuable office space. Plans were underway to purchase a newer, bigger building in anticipation of company expansion. In the interim, Brendan had placed these files in our garage as a temporary storage area until a bigger corporate building could be leased or purchased. They were only supposed to be stored here for one month. But that transaction had never transpired, so the boxes remained in our garage. Brendan had requested that Mark retrieve the boxes should Brendan's illness take a turn for the worse. But Mark became overwhelmed with responsibilities in Brendan's absence and had not been able to find the time to drop by to pick them up.

But now that the kids were getting bigger, so were their toys—skateboards, surfboards, bikes, etc.—and the garage was in dire need of a purge.

I decided to breeze through the files and make sure they pertained entirely to Zander before having them sent to Mark. The boxes were stacked in two tiers, so the first eight boxes that were not stacked so high were easy to inspect. Using the stepladder to get to the boxes that were stacked higher, I began to tug at the topmost file box when the tip of my nail snapped off and my finger started to bleed. Struggling to hold onto the box with one hand, it toppled to the ground leaving the entire contents strewn all over the floor. I cursed, climbed down the ladder, walked to the bathroom to clean my finger, and applied a bandage.

I returned to the garage to gather the contents of the file and place them back in the box, sorting and organizing, until I stumbled upon canceled checks made out to Trevor English.

69

HATE TO SEE YOUR HEARTBREAK

As I drove down PCH towards Laguna Beach, I thought about Trevor. I had thought about him many times over the years. I wondered if he was still playing music, or if he had gotten married. But now I was wondering why my late husband wrote checks to Trevor over a period of four years, beginning one week before Trevor's audition for Scarlet White.

On a whim, I took a chance to see if Trevor still lived at the same cottage in Laguna Beach. It had been just over fifteen years when I saw him last, and I realized that the likelihood of his still living in that cottage would be a shot in the dark. Nevertheless, this would at least be the first step in tracking him down.

Feeling somewhat apprehensive, I parked across the street and sat in my car for a moment. Trevor had lived in the second cottage in a row of four identical cottages—all painted the same pale yellow, gray, and periwinkle. I observed the house for a few moments trying to recollect any specific characteristics on the outside that spoke of Trevor. I saw two potted plants, just like before, but I think the plants themselves were different. Of course changes would be inevitable after fifteen years.

I rang the doorbell and waited. It was 9:00 a.m. If Trevor was the same Trevor as he was sixteen years ago, he would have a hangover, and it would take him a while to climb out of bed to answer the door on a Sunday morning. I rang the doorbell again and heard rumbling from within. A few seconds later the front door opened. It was dark inside, and I couldn't make out who was standing across the screen door. But he could see me in the light. "Margee, is that you, or am I looking at a ghost?"

I recognized the accent. "Hello, Trevor."

"Oh, my God."

"I'm so sorry to spring up on you with no notice. I hope this isn't a bad time."

Trevor opened the door. "Oh my God. Come in. Crikey, Margee. What on earth?"

"I know. I can't believe you still live here. I guess I got lucky. Are you alone? I don't want to impose."

"Well, I do have a lady in my bedroom right now, but it's okay. Darla! Come here, girl… meet my long lost friend!" A few seconds later, a lovely little lady entered the room. Waddling gingerly, an elderly stout Welsh corgi appeared through Trevor's bedroom door, yawning. As she approached, the nub of her tail wagged slowly.

"Meet my girlfriend." A light shone from Trevor's heart.

"Awww, she's beautiful!" I knelt down to greet her. "You always did like the older girls."

"She's my sweetheart—fourteen years old. I adopted her seven years ago from the corgi rescue."

I patted Darla gently and scratched her neck. Then, all of a sudden, another creature jumped down from a desk and approached me. She was a fat, black and white cat with a masked face like the markings of a raccoon. Her fur, though she stood too far away from me to stroke her, appeared to be soft, silky and thick, like a bunny's. Her eyes were open wide with youth and curiosity. I admired her and said hello. Darla went to sniff her, and she bopped Darla on the nose with her paw.

"Sasha, that's not nice," Trevor scolded.

"Do I at least get a hug?" I asked.

"Of course you do."

Trevor embraced me for an unusually long while. He released me, and his eyes held mine. "Margee, it's great to see you again."

Sixteen years was a long time, but he was still the same Trevor, only older and in great shape. I noticed a new tattoo on the lower half of his left arm—a tribal design. It reminded me of a Maori warrior tattoo I'd seen on a documentary.

We caught up briefly with each other's lives. He was freelancing, updating a software application for Apple, which enabled musicians to create and write music on the computer. He mentioned that he was writing music for theater productions and jingles as well.

Trevor's place had changed since the last time I visited. He had remodeled the kitchen with soapstone countertops and a large apron sink. A black leather swivel chair took center stage in the living room, surrounded by wall-to-wall electronic equipment, including four keyboards, recording equipment, a twenty-seven inch computer monitor, and a great piece of modern art on the wall. At his desk wall, I noticed something familiar. I walked over to take a closer look. It was our old Scarlet White photo, walking in the snowfall, beautifully framed. And just below it was another photograph of Scarlet White, live on stage.

"Was this at Bogart's?"

"Good memory."

I sighed, sentimentally, and continued to gaze.

"Scarlet White," Trevor expressed nostalgically, "by far the best band I've ever had the privilege to be a part of."

I cast a quiet smile. "The place looks great, Trevor. I'm glad that you still live in same house. Otherwise I would have had to track you down."

"I own all the units now. I bought them five years ago and rent out the other ones. I kept thinking about moving to a bigger place, but it's convenient. I do all the handyman work for the tenants, so I don't have to go far to fix anything if I stay here. Got everything I need right here. So what's going on with you, Margee? What brings you here after all this time?"

"Brendan passed away last year."

"I'm so sorry to hear that."

I looked at Trevor for a few moments and decided to drop the bomb. "You knew him. When I introduced Brendan to the band at the Vixen, you had already met him. You were on his payroll, but you never worked at Urban Perspective. Brendan was writing personal checks to you." I presented the canceled checks. "Why don't you tell me what this is all about Trevor?"

Trevor took a seat and offered me one. He hesitated as if gathering his thoughts and words. His eyes met mine and then turned away. He shook his head, let out a long sigh, and rubbed his face with both hands. "I was hired to play in a band with you."

"Brendan hired you to play keyboards for us? But why would Brendan feel a need to do that?"

"Brendan wanted to find out more about you. Did you have a boyfriend? Were you promiscuous? Did you do drugs? What did you do after the shows? What other interests did you have besides music? That sort of thing—all sorts of things..."

I was baffled by this information.

"Were you Brendan's spy?"

"Margee, it was a long time ago. I was young and trying to put myself through college. It was easy money. It seemed harmless. He told me he just wanted to really know the woman he was going to marry before he put in the extra effort to make a lifelong commitment. I know it sounds strange, but if you think about it, it *is* a reasonable thing to want. I just thought, hey, if I had the money, I might like to check out a person before making a lifelong commitment. Fair enough. He wasn't hurting anyone. I wasn't hurting anyone."

"But he already knew me. We worked together. We had lunch together. I don't get it."

"Brendan Knight was looking for a life partner," Trevor explained. "He wanted to know *everything* about you. I don't know if you can find out about a person by simply having lunch with them on occasion. And you refused to date anyone back then, right? He wanted to know whether you were worth fighting for, I suppose. Then he stopped needing me when you became pregnant and engaged, but he kept sending me checks to keep me quiet for the next two years. Then the checks stopped coming. I guess he figured his secret was safe since you quit the band, and we lost contact."

The entire exposé was puzzling. *People just don't do that*, I thought. But then, what Trevor said was true. I wouldn't date Brendan for the longest time. And Brendan, as Stacey said, always got what he wanted. Then I thought about the punctures in the condoms. *Had Brendan already decided we were to be married before we became an official couple?*

Trevor stood up and retrieved a folded piece of paper from a wooden keepsake box on his desk. "Brendan paid me a visit several months ago. He asked me to give you this note if you ever found out about my relationship with him."

"Trevor, did Brendan ever know about us?"

"No. I never said a word."

My head was spinning. I got up abruptly and said goodbye to Trevor.

"Margee, wait!"

Confused and hurt, I turned around and looked at Trevor. I wanted to read the letter and couldn't wait another minute.

"I'm truly sorry," Trevor apologized. "I wanted to tell you, Margee, after the ostrich attack. Remember that time, the last day that you took care of me? When you left, you kissed me on the cheek. I wanted to tell you at that very moment. And the two times we were together. I can't tell you how much I wanted to tell you. Finally, I thought, bloody hell, I'm going to tell her what's going on. It was beginning to feel so wrong. But the last time we spoke, you were carrying his baby, and you said you were going to marry him. You told me you loved him."

After all these years, Trevor had set all his accursed secrets free. I could see him, right down to the depth of his soul, and I knew he was genuinely sorry. But I was confused. I didn't know at that moment how to process the information. My eyes were beginning to well.

"Margee—"

"It's just… it's too much, Trevor. I need some time. I have to go now."

I drove a short distance from Trevor's cottage and parked my car. Gazing at the letter with uncertainty, I unfolded and read it.

Dear Margee,

For too many years I've kept a secret and carried an ocean of guilt along with it. I couldn't imagine a life without you, and in my desperation and selfishness, I robbed you of your life's dream. It was only after the fact, when I saw how deeply it hurt you, did I realize what a terrible thing I had done. As the years passed, I thought of telling you the truth so many times, but I was afraid that if I did, I'd lose you forever and break up our beautiful family. And that was something I was unwilling to risk. I'm truly sorry for what I've done.

Though I didn't live a long life, I lived a perfect life because of you. I want you to be happy now, Margee. Give my girl, Bronny, and my best man, Jude, a big long hug.

I will love you for all eternity.

Brendan

I closed my eyes, pressed the letter to my chest, and wept.

70

TWO WEEKS LATER

Laguna Beach is always beautiful, warm, and clear as its wealthy residents "can easily afford to pay their weather bill". I had heard Randy make this comment many times in jest. But the longer I lived in SoCal, the more it seemed to be true. Even if it's raining in the borderline cities, it's always sunny in Laguna Beach.

I met Sanjoy for lunch at the Montage. It was his birthday, so I treated him to lobster bisque and a compressed arugula pistachio salad. Of late, Sanjoy ping-ponged from one diet to the next in an effort to tame his middle-aged midsection. Once, I jokingly told him he was getting a little bit too fat and sassy, and the comment ruffled his feathers so much that I had to shower him with compliments before he would return to his normal semi-arrogant disposition. Since then, I had been very careful with my words.

"I'm on a new, low-carbohydrate, high-protein diet," he explained.

"So you can't eat that lovely puff pastry covering your bisque, but you can have flan for dessert and four glasses of wine. That's a great diet," I teased.

During our lunch, I brought up the events that took place at the Vixen. "Sanjoy, I'm sorry for pushing you away all those years. I didn't know the truth back then, but now I do. I know Lori didn't sabotage the sound system that day. It was Brendan."

"Margee, I wish you could have heard her. She swore up and down that she didn't do it. She was so adamant about it. And she saw Brendan enter the Vixen after she left."

"I know Sanjoy. She was telling the truth. But at the time, all the evidence pointed towards her. And I felt like you betrayed me by continuing to associate with her. I felt like you took her side, because you cared more about having a celebrity friend than a true blue friend. But you were just caught in the middle. Anyway, if you see her, tell her it's okay. I mean, she did take my songs, but I wasn't going to do anything with those songs anyway. At least she gave them life and shared them with the world."

Sanjoy accepted my apology only after giving me grief about how he missed out on watching my kids grow up. I missed out too. I was lonely, and I would have loved having Sanjoy be a part of my life. How foolish I had been for not seeing how green the grass already was on my side of the fence.

71

TALK OF THE TOWN

At half past noon, on a gray, May Thursday, the doorbell rang unexpectedly. Typically, visitors at our front door were neighborhood kids calling on Bronwyn or Jude. I wasn't expecting a visitor, and solicitors didn't typically come to our door. They would have had to pass through the tall front gate first, which feels like an intrusion of private property for most people.

In the middle of chopping vegetables for jambalaya, I washed and wiped my hands to answer the door. The next few moments would be engraved in my memory for a lifetime as I stood there, stunned by the woman standing in front of me. I had seen her many times through the years on magazine covers at nearly every grocery stand. Her face was familiar to millions worldwide. She was an icon and the target of hungry paparazzi. She was the cover girl, seen on TV commercials endorsing makeup and hair products for multibillion-dollar cosmetic companies. And she was the idol my daughter continued to worship. Here she stood, the rock goddess, with a baby olive tree in one shaking hand.

Finally, in a voice that sounded rich and deeper than I remembered, she asked, "Margee McGuire, do you think we can talk like two civilized women now?"

I stood there as the moments passed, dumbfounded, mouth open, as she waited for a response.

 "Are you going to ask me to come in? Or should I leave?"

I let out a sigh. "Yes, no, I mean, please come in. I…it's just that this is so unexpected."

"I'm sorry for showing up unannounced."

"Oh, no. Don't be sorry. It's okay—really."

She mentioned that she had just come off a tour and had some time off. Her eyes traveled around our great room. "Oh my God. This is a *really* nice place you have here." She recognized a painting that Brendan had bought me for my 40th birthday. "Is this a Miro?"

"Yes, it is."

"I like Miro." She admired a second painting. "This is a nice piece too."

"He's a new artist from Los Angeles. His name is Mukherjee. Would you like something to drink—a glass of wine?"

"I'd love a glass of wine. You haven't changed. I'm glad," she responded with a smile, but still with eyes of uncertainty.

I opened a special bottle of Grand Cru Bordeaux Saint Emilion that Brendan had brought back from France several years ago, awaiting a special occasion. She inquired about Bronwyn and Jude, and I shared photos. I told her about Bronwyn's obsession with her. As we conversed, I couldn't help but notice how beautiful she was. Even though the years had slowly begun to claim her, Lori was blessed with great facial bone structure. I had thought that the road and her appetite for parties would have aged her twice as fast. Even though she had a few lines around the corners of her eyes, she was beautiful. She appeared healthy, without very much makeup.

"Lori, time has only made you more beautiful. What's your secret?"

"I had that close call a few years ago," she explained. "You may have heard about it. It was all over the news. Anyway, I decided to clean up my act. But those first five years, I was living life in the fast lane. You know how I was, Margee."

"Yeah...I remember. You could party every night of the week."

"Not many people are privy to this, but when I OD'ed, I had that outer body experience thing happen. I left my body and looked down at my dying body."

"I've heard of that happening to people."

"Yeah...pretty trippy. Anyway, to make a long story short, that experience changed everything. I thought about my life. And, I thought about you many times, Margee. I thought about how you would have never wasted your life like me. I thought about how much in control you were with your life, how hard you worked and dedicated yourself, and how disciplined you were. And it began to sink in. I have a purpose. And if I'm going to survive, I have to change my way of living. I decided that I was going to make the best out of my life like you would have, had you been given my gift. So I turned my life around. I laid low for a while... to avoid the negative media. Then after another year of getting my act together, I decided to make a comeback. So here I am. No more drugs. Just fine wine." She winked and held up her glass, and we clinked our glasses like we had done so many times before.

We continued to talk about old times for the next hour or so, when I realized that this was probably the last time I would see her. "Lori, I just want to say I'm sorry..."

But she held up her hand and shook her head side-to-side. "No need. But I will tell you, my friend, the last time I saw you, you broke my fucking nose. They had to set it back in place and reconstruct it, and then it took eight months before I was able to sing again." She chuckled.

I put my hand up to my mouth in horror, then we both busted out in laughter.

"Dude, do you even know how painful it was?" she added. "I had two black eyes, and my nose was over here." She placed one finger on the side of her face, and we laughed until our laughter escalated to tears.

When I gained composure, I asked, "When the dust settled, why didn't you tell me you didn't do it, Lori?"

"You wouldn't have believed me. And then the next time I saw Sanjoy, he told me you were pregnant and that you were going to marry Brendan, so Sanjoy and I both thought that maybe it would be best for me to carry the blame forever. Sanjoy wasn't sure who to believe at first. But I swore up and down to him that I didn't do it, and I finally convinced him. I was able to put the pieces together when I remembered seeing Brendan walk into the Vixen as I left the parking lot that day. At the time, I didn't think anything of it. I thought maybe you forgot something. And Brendan... Who would have ever thought in a million years, a person so dignified in every regard would do something like that? Then the news came that Brendan passed away, and Sanjoy said you didn't have hard feelings anymore towards me. Anyway, Brendan must have loved you in a desperate way to do what he did."

"I suppose," I said. "But I have such conflicting feelings about it. Love isn't really supposed to be selfish like that. I try not to think about it too much."

We fell silent for a few moments.

"Lori, I appreciate that you took time out of your schedule to visit."

"There is a specific reason I came here, Margee. I want to somehow make it up to you. I took your songs. I want to set this right—"

"I don't need the money, Lori. I have plenty of money. One day, when they write a book about your life, maybe you can mention something about me. How great I am at head-butting!"

We fell silent again for a few moments as I detected a slight mist in her eyes, when suddenly the door flung open delivering Bronwyn and Jude.

"Hi Mom, I'm hungry," Bronwyn announced. "What do you have to eat? Hey Mom, you won't believe what happened to me today."

"No Bronz, *you* won't believe what happened to me today."

Bronwyn lifted her head and zeroed in on Lori's face. In two seconds, Bronwyn's face transformed. She had the oddest expression: a combination of disbelief and confusion settling into eventual wonder. Lori and I busted out in laughter.

"You guys must be Bronwyn and Jude," Lori said with a huge smile.

But Bronwyn just stood there looking goofy and confused.

"No way," Jude uttered.

"Guys, say hello to Lourdes Love!" I resounded.

Bronwyn dropped her backpack and placed her hands over her mouth.

"Oh my God," she whispered.

Lori stood up, walked over to Bronwyn, and gave her and Jude a big hug.

Bronwyn, for the first time in her life, could not think about eating. I continued to remind her that she had volleyball practice and should eat, but the energy that was racing through her body as she sat next to Lourdes Love had completely conquered her appetite. Lori shared stories of her concerts, other famous celebrities, and an acting role in a major motion picture due to hit the theaters in late November, while Bronwyn drank in every drop like sipping a passion fruit smoothie on a searing hot day. Two hours flew by, and we were already ten minutes late for Bronwyn's volleyball practice. I contemplated having her skip altogether, but her team had a statewide tournament in two days and Bronwyn was team captain. To have her play hooky and claim that Lourdes Love was visiting would not have been plausible.

"We really should be going, Lori," I said.

"I have to head out anyway. I'll give her a ride."

As Lori and Bronwyn walked to Lori's Aston Martin, Lori placed her arm around Bronwyn's shoulder, and in the distance I could hear Lori speaking. "Did you know that your mother was all the rage when she played the Orange County/L.A. circuit. Hold on for just one minute. I almost forgot. I have something I need to give to your mom."

Lori returned, pulled an object out of her pocket, and handed it to me. "Margee, please do me a huge favor and find the person this belongs to and tell her I'm sorry."

I viewed the object and gave Lori a puzzled look.

"I was given a second chance at life. Before I can go forward, I have to try to make the things that I've done wrong, right." Lori turned to join Bronwyn. I gazed at the object in my hand. It was a beautiful necklace on a 24-carat gold chain that held a jade cross with a stamped lace back and a gold medallion on the front crest.

72

SOMEWHERE ONLY WE KNOW

I t was a cool spring morning as the sun glimmered through the jacaranda trees at Newport Memorial Cemetery. They were in full bloom, and the purple petals above the green lawn against the blue skies were stunning. I looked down upon my finger at the gold twist tie, a treasured keepsake that took residence in a special place in my jewelry box for years after I had gotten my wedding ring. But the gold twist tie always brought a smile to my face. Each time I visited Brendan, I wore it. I had made it a ritual to visit Brendan's gravesite nearly every Sunday morning with the kids, but both were visiting their grandparents in Connecticut. Anyway, on this day, I wanted to be alone, because I felt the need to speak to Brendan, heart-to-heart. I inhaled a lilac sprig and placed it on his plaque.

"I'm okay now, Brendan. I was angry for a long time. And I know somehow, in your world, you must know how angry you made me. But now... I think you know, that I *don't* blame you anymore... I love you... I will always love you. We created

Bronwyn and Jude, and I can't imagine a life without them. Lori may have fame and fortune, but she doesn't have what I have, and I wouldn't change my life even if I could. I wouldn't change a thing. So, I want you to know that I have no regrets. We miss you. We miss you *so* much."

Walking back to my car, I saw a dog in the distance. It was strange to see a dog in the cemetery without an owner. He was jumping around, chasing after a butterfly. Suddenly, he looked at me and wore a smile on his face. He wagged his tail and disappeared into the trees.

73

GOOD RIDDANCE

Jermaine, our twelve-month-old teenage cat, was waiting at the door for me. I decided to feed him, even though he needed to go on a diet soon. He was three pounds overweight, and I had been trying to feed him less often. When he thinks he's hungry, and he always thinks he's hungry, he starts licking my toes, a strange habit of his. It feels rough, yet ticklish, and I hadn't quite figured out how to make him stop, so I usually put him in a short time-out in the garage. But today I was alone and I wanted his company. So I gave him a snack.

I had two messages on my answering machine.

(Message 1)

Hi Mom, it's Bronz. Just calling to see how you're doing. Guess what we did today? We played golf, and I am the bomb! Granddad said I remind him of you. Anyway, I'll call you tomorrow. Love you. Hey, Jude! Tell Mom hi...
Hi, Mom! I love you. Can't talk. I'm playing LOL.

(Message 2)

Hello, Margee, it's Trevor. Just calling to check up on you. I'm in your neck of the woods Friday, and I was hoping you'd be free to have dinner. (Pause) It was really good to see you again...really good. Call me, I would love to hear from you.

I took in a deep breath and tranquility engulfed me. The cool night breeze that flowed through the kitchen window was invigorating. I thought about the dog at the cemetery and traveled deep into the historical file cabinet in my mind—Jack and Ellie. I didn't waste a year with them. What I experienced back then could never be recreated, when you consider the laughter, the music, the freedom, and the southern ambiance at that run-down shack on Alcovy Road. I continued to reminisce, and I wondered why some of us can't understand that the good old days are being created each day as we live our lives in the company of our loved ones. And those little things, like the dog and butterfly—which brought not only joy to the heart in the most pure and simplistic way—had messages that carry great significance as they carve the path towards our destiny and weave the magnificent tapestry of our lives.

As I sat on the sofa, I became transfixed by a framed photograph of Bronwyn and Jude—a selfie Bronwyn had taken just two weeks ago at the beach. She had it enlarged and cropped. Thoughtfully, she framed it and gave it to me before they left for Connecticut. "Here, Mom. I know you'll miss us, so I made this for you."

It was a close-up, cheek-to-cheek photo. I couldn't help but smile. Then I noticed something I had never noticed before—something different, something new about Bronwyn. Suddenly, it hit me, smack in the face. I took the framed photograph and held it in my hand to examine it closely. And it wasn't my imagination. In her sparkling amber eyes were little dark specks. As I continued to gaze at the photo, a flood of memories, like little pieces of a puzzle, began to fall into place. Bronwyn was born nearly three weeks late. At the time, I thought nothing of it. Brendan had left no stone unturned. He must have punctured the condoms that were in my personal possession. He knew I carried one in my purse for insurance, because I could never be "too careful". Bronwyn grew to be tall and slender. She held her back straight and her head high. But the specks were so undeniably unique. I had lost myself in those eyes before, and his eyes were exactly the same. It was uncanny. So much so, I felt a chill. And so, the last piece of the puzzle fell into place, as I gazed into those unforgettable eyes—topaz islands on amber planets.

EPILOGUE

n the game of life, those who make and break the rules don't always win. Or perhaps they don't win within the terms they had imagined.

As for Brendan, he left this world believing he had accomplished and obtained what he had sought. In reality, his picture wasn't perfect. His not knowing the truth secured his happiness, and on the highest level, he was still a father to two loving children. He married the woman of his dreams. He created a successful business. He wins.

I wonder where Lori's life would be had we never met. The first occupation that pops into my mind: waitress. Instead, she accomplished a dream. From her haphazard lifestyle, the impossible dream. With a slight twist of fate and the help of an inconceivable accomplice, she took a chance, reached up to the stars, and ended up in a place she could have only imagined in her *wildest* dreams. She wins.

As I reflect on my past, I realize that how you define failure and success in life is simply a matter of perspective. Sometimes in order to win, you have to sacrifice something. I never reached the goal I originally sought, but through my intervention, somebody else's dream came true. That makes me, and others like me, extraordinary. Fame does not stop on our street, glory does not rain on our garden, and our story may be unsung. But we have a purpose and a calling. If you're a lucky charm like me, with the briefest of moments in the limelight, when suddenly your life takes a turn, and your dreams are blown away like the petals of a dandelion in a swift summer breeze, accept the gifts that are behind that secret door, and know beyond the shadow of a doubt that you are an intricate and fundamental player in this grand game of life. Count your blessings every day, because how you accept what providence has bestowed upon you is merely a matter of character. I win.

The End

ACKNOWLEDGMENTS

A special thanks to my dear friend, Debbie Moore Wasikowski, who restored my faith in myself and for being the friend who graciously accepted the task of editing my book in the early (grueling) stages when my manuscript was twice as long. Debbie expressed so much enthusiasm when she finished reading my manuscript. It validated the worthiness of my story and propelled me to continue to improve. From that moment on, she was my vision keeper for seeing this through.

A shower of gratitude to Lorraine Buell for her encouragement and for sharing her knowledge of creative writing. Even though she had both hands full, she managed to find the time to coach me through the first thirty pages. Her suggestions and direction set me in motion to revamp my entire novel for the better.

There are few people in my life whose friendship and faith in me was unwavering. In my most dire time of need, Ekta Karnani was the one who stepped up with ferocious intentions of standing by me every step of the way. She was the friend I could count on, and she made me believe I could manifest anything my heart desires. I'm grateful that our paths crossed so long ago, and I finally understand the meaning of "kindred spirits".

How could I have written this book without the boys in the band? There were several throughout the years, and of course some stood out more than others. They made my life anything but boring.

I want to express my gratitude to my editors, Lynette Smith and Andrea Glass, for their support, attention to detail, and encouragement—all delivered with patience and kindness.

Thanks to the monkeys at Monkey C Media: Jeniffer Thompson, Kat Endries, Chad Thompson, Ella Joyce, Lilli Kendle, and Julio Pompa for turning my vision into reality.

I was fortunate to grow up with three unique brothers: Lenny Andrews, Bill Andrews, and Perry Andrews. At some point in my life they took me in when I had little money and no place to go. I'm forever grateful for their love and protection.

I am always in awe of how my mother survived war, hunger, slavery, and a heartbreaking divorce. Rather than choosing to be a victim, she chose to be courageous. And it is to her credit that I became strong physically and spiritually. I inherited my gift of intuition from her. And when I finally realized it was real, my eyes opened up to a whole new world. She once said, "When I leave this earth, all you have to do is think of me, and I be right by your side so fast, faster than airplane, faster than lightning—zoon! I be there." Whether in the physical or spiritual realm, I will always look to her for guidance and strength.

When my father wrote his story, he inspired me to write mine. It was the best gift I could ever give to myself. It gives me serenity knowing there is nothing but unconditional love in heaven where his soul lives on.

ABOUT THE AUTHOR

Suzan Marion McClelland has spent over three decades of her life as a songwriter and alternative rock musician in Southern California performing in the Orange County and Los Angeles area. She began writing *Scarlet White* in 2010 while raising her family and working as a fitness/wellness coach. *Scarlet White* is Suzan's first novel.

Follow Suzan: Facebook.com/suzanmarionmcclelland